# AN ORDI
# MAN . . . .

To the countless numbers of other ordinary
men and women of my generation who may
recognise a little of themselves in me

## OTHER TITLES BY THE SAME AUTHOR

◆

CHRISTMAS ISLAND,
THE WRONG PLACE AT THE WRONG TIME

First Published 1997 by Minerva Press
2nd Impression 1998 by Minerva Press
3rd Impression 2002 by UPFRONT PUBLISHING

◆

TIDE OF FORTUNE - TIME OF CHANGE

First Published 2000 by Minerva Press
2nd Edition 2002 by UPFRONT PUBLISHING

Published by Printability Publishing on behalf of Jim Haggas ©.
Designed & Printed by Atkinson Print Ltd.
10/11 Lower Church Street, Hartlepool TS24 7DJ
Tel: 01429 267849 Fax: 01429 865416 ISDN No: 01429 894231
e-mail: printability@atkinsonprint.co.uk www.atkinsonprint.co.uk
ISBN 1 872239 43 9

# CONTENTS

# INTRODUCTION

Like millions of others of my generation I lay no particular claim to fame. I haven't climbed every mountain, forded every stream nor followed every rainbow. Neither have I had a wish to do so. My achievements have been less than modest by most measures of recognition. No plaque will mark the house I was born in. I was not born into any great wealth neither will I leave any. In the grand opera of life I have rarely been cast in a leading role. I have strutted and fretted my hour upon the stage more often than not as one of the supporting cast. In short, a man doing ordinary things at ordinary times in ordinary places. More humdrum than humming, the full story of my life would not be regarded as a stimulating read but it has had it's moments and sometimes it's modest accomplishments. The satisfaction of a few acceptable buildings as an Architect perhaps and the realisation of a couple of interesting books as a writer. Who knows, maybe the ordinary lives of the many are in some ways more rewarding than the famous lives of the few. Ironically enough neither will ever know.

None the worse for having spent their formative years in the make do and mend years of the second world war, and living under the menacing clouds of a cold war which mercifully did not turn into the more deadly mushroom clouds of a nuclear holocaust, I have no doubt that I and my generation were surely born in the right place at the right time. Whilst many parts of the world have had the worst fifty years in their history, we have enjoyed a half century of European peace whilst reaping the benefits of a half century of scientific and technological progress for the first time in our history. Ushered in with the fabulous fifties, nurtured by the swinging sixties, cushioned by a welfare state and ironically enough latterly aided and abetted by the covert designs of an ambitious but misguided European Parliament, the atomic age has also seen a huge change in the way our society lives.

In his time, Prime Minister Harold Wilson promised a new Britain 'forged in the heat of a scientific revolution', but few could have forecast at the time just how markedly different the way of life in that new Britain of the future would be forged. In the past fifty years we have seen extensive - the more perceptive would claim alarming - changes in our philosophy, values and standards. As we slip ever lower down the European league of merit in just about everything, we have witnessed malicious attempts to denigrate our heroes and furtive efforts to re-evaluate our very history. At a time when our way of life is being changed and changed in a manner and at a pace that it has never been changed before, we choose to imitate the actions of the ostrich and bury our heads in the sand. Sadly enough, my generation is too advanced in years to take any effective action now, and the younger generation appears too immature - or too unconcerned - to recognise that there is any need to do so before our heritage slips into oblivion. It will be for the future historians to record the how's, the why's and the wherefores of the transformation of our society, but history will show whether the changes in the past half century will eventually prove for the greater and the good of future generations.

I have discovered that views are often sought from people because they are famous rather than because they are famous for their views. They are seldom if ever sought if they are neither. If three weeks on crutches following a less fortunate sporting accident shortly before retiring was the catalyst for my late entry into authorship, then writing was the more fortunate outcome during my retirement. After a lifetime in the all time and thought consuming practice of Architecture both in my home town and abroad, I realised that I had things to say in a way I wished to say them, comments to make in a way I wished to make them, stories to tell in a way I wished to tell them and experiences to share in a way I wished to share them. More importantly for the first time in my life I had the time to tell them. I believe we should tell it as it is rather than believe those who would have us believe it is, and I would like to think that controversial or otherwise, my views where I have expressed them, are shared by many if not by most of my generation. Some readers may even recognise a little of themselves in me. Perhaps the book should have been called 'Just Like You'.

The book is based on my own views and personal recollections, some of which are more distant than others. I'm sure one of the first accomplishments of a writer is to keep a long story short, but since there is no knowledge which is not valuable, I hope I will be excused for including a little history and a few hard facts and figures where I considered these to be relevant. The kaleidoscope of articles gathered together here have been written at various times shortly before and since my retirement, in the hope that they will evoke memories of people and places both past and present for many of my generation, possibly serve as a wake up call for some of our more outrageous transgressions of and on our society, and hopefully provide a sound bite of the past for the generations of the future. I have included a few extracts from my last two books, which relate the story of some of the more unusual and sometimes more disturbing of my experiences, and I have attempted to place all the stories into some form of chronological order. A short introduction to each of the stories has been added by way of explanation, and the photographs and sketches which supplement my writing will I hope both amuse and help to paint a picture of a way of life which in so many ways has already been consigned to the pages of the last century. Whilst I wish to get my point across I have no wish to stab anyone with it, but I have my own views about what is right and what is wrong. In a society which now believes what was wrong then is right now, and what is wrong now was right then, the readers must decide for themselves just what has been consigned for better or worse.

I like to think that we gain a little something from each and every person we meet as we journey through life and by way of acknowledgement I have to recognise a host of past fellow travellers who are far too numerous to mention here. I have to thank my parents for their willing sacrifices in giving me the best of starts in life and smoothing my passage from child to adulthood. I did not ask to be born, nor did I ask to be born in the place or at the time I was, but I do look back upon my own childhood and realise just how fortunate I have been.

I should like to thank Neil for his help with my computer and the assistance of my wife June who has always supported my endeavours. Once again I have to thank her for encouraging me to incorporate this series of articles into book form and sustaining me during the preparation of it. I hope it will bring back a few memories for the reader - not too painful ones I trust - and perhaps serve as a reminder that despite the undoubted benefits that technology may have brought, the British way of life is being slowly undermined, and all is not as well as it could be, or indeed as it should be, in today's beleagued society.

# 1. A CLEAN FRONT STEP

*To live through an entire century is a remarkable achievement. To be born only a year after the death of Queen Victoria as one of millions of actors on the world stage and witness the incredible changes that have taken place throughout the twentieth century is even more remarkable. My mother has lived through the reign of five monarchs from Edward 7th to Elizabeth 2nd, and the governments of nineteen Prime Ministers from James Balfour to Tony Blair. Born in Edwardian England at a time when Brittania ruled the waves and the sun literally never set on a British Empire which covered a fifth of the earth's surface, she has lived through two world wars and a great deal of global unrest. From the franchise for women to the Welfare State, from horse carriages to concord and silent movies to digital television, she has been privileged to witness the huge advances in equality and technology that have brought such a significant change in our lifestyle.*

*To mark the occasion I wrote this story a few months before her one hundredth birthday.*

I visited my mother again earlier today. I do so every day of the week now. God willing she will be one hundred years old in October this year and with the help of a walking frame and the reassurance of an emergency call pendant which hangs around her neck, she still lives on her own in a one bedroom ground floor flat in Hemlington. My father who died over thirty years ago of chronic bronchitis, largely as a result of service in the trenches during the first world war, used to say that she was one in a million. When she does reach her century she probably will be. Like her mother before her she has a fierce determination to maintain standards, 'I like to keep the place clean and tidy'. Like most of her generation she is a proud lady who values her independence. 'I wouldn't survive long in a nursing home', she says knowingly and I believe this to be true. As her only son I am her official carer. 'As long as you can use the bathroom, dress yourself and make the odd cup of tea you are fine here', I reply by way of encouragement. 'I've lived so long and met so many people I could write a book about my life', she says. I say, 'Tell me about it and I'll write the book for you'.

Her mother died in childbirth with her tenth child. As the first born of a surviving family of six children living in a small rented two bedroom terrace house in Ayre Street in Middlesbrough, she was cast early in the role of mother figure. 'It was customary to have a large family in those days. The youngest was only a baby when mother died. I took good care of them. Children know when they're loved and wanted you know'. Life cannot have been easy. 'The two boys slept in the front room with my mother and father and I slept with the girls in the larger back bedroom'. Ironically she has survived them all. 'We didn't have a lot of money. We baked our own bread and my mother taught me how to knead the dough. All the clothes were handed down. Dad had a last to repair the children's shoes on and I used to darn their socks. I was so thrilled when he bought me my first new dress and I wore it when we walked in Albert Park after church service on a Sunday. We couldn't afford any holidays but once or twice a year we went for a day out. We used to take the tram which ran down Parliament Road to the station and went to Redcar on the train. It seemed such a long journey in those days but it was so thrilling and we all looked forward to it so much that we couldn't sleep the night before'. On some things she is more guarded. 'Mother never seemed to have the time to talk to me. She had so much to do. I missed out on my teenage years. I had no time to flirt with the boys like the others. There was a lot of questions I would have liked to have asked my mother and I knew nothing until I met your dad. My friend Florrie was always asking me to go somewhere but I hadn't the time'.

When June and I take her to the shops at the weekend she wears dark glasses. She says she doesn't like to be seen in her wheelchair but I tell her that there are few of her past friends left to see her in it. She's given up reading the newspapers because she says they're all bad news. 'What a nasty place the world is now. What is the world coming to. People don't go to church anymore do they and whatever has happened to family life. There's so much violence nowadays. There is no respect for the law anymore and nobody seems to be punished. If I could get out on my own where could I safely walk to now without being attacked'.
She's right of course. She comes from a more trustworthy generation that left the front door open for the family doctor to walk in, and a the latch key on a string behind the letter box for the family and anyone else to do the same. A generation which held basic values of decency, honour and trust and a sense of national identity in a national community. Mindful of the ever increasing lawless acts and gratuitous violence in today's materialistic society, which panders to the misplaced notion of behavioural treatment for criminals rather than a regard for the safety of the public or any form of

punishment, few would disagree with her. How long before we stop turning the other cheek. How long I wonder before society wakes up to the fact that we are rapidly losing the battle against crime. How long before victims of crime start to take their own vengeance, and how long before vigilante groups resolve to seek their own justice against those they consider to have committed unspeakable offences. Elected members of a democratic Government ignore such matters at their peril.

Sometimes I look across the table whilst we are having a meal and I have to remind myself that she is almost one hundred years old. She certainly doesn't look it. Perhaps it was all the walking she did throughout her life. She was going on holiday with a friend in her eighties and when her friend passed on she went by herself in her nineties. 'They got me on to the stage one holiday and I sang Nellie Dean', and she throws her head back and breaks into hesitant song, 'There's an old mill by the stream....' When she went into hospital for the first time in her life a couple of years ago for a minor operation on her leg, the nurses refused to believe her age. Time stops for no man, yet strangely enough while she is around I feel little sense of my own mortality. I'm retired myself now, and I trust that I will inherit my mother's good health and vitality into old age. Maybe the family genes will take care of it.
Her hairdresser appears once a month to wash and set her tousled silvering hair over the kitchen sink, 'it was far too hot under the hair dryer this morning', and the chiropodist calls whenever a particular painful corn causes trouble, 'I'm glad when she's gone. I can't stand to look you know. I think all my nerves must be in my feet'. She looks vulnerable at times, but I recognise her frustration at not being able to walk unaided. The doctor tells her that this is due to her age but I don't believe she really accepts this. 'I want to do things but my body won't let me do them. I know I'm not twenty one any more'. At other times she gets a little depressed. 'The time goes so quickly. Where does it go. I seem to spend most of my time getting up and getting dressed, and getting undressed to go back to bed again these days. Other than the family what have I got to live for', she will say. Better to wear out than to rust out I ruse. 'Your hundredth birthday for one thing and a telegram from the Queen for another', I reply before checking her prescription to make sure she has been taking her daily pills in the correct order, 'there are always those worse off than yourself you know'.

She insists on making some meals herself but I worry about her using the gas cooker when I'm not there. Finding a variety of 'boil in the bag' and other convenience foods is always a problem, and there is a limit to what she can manage to do. Opening packaged food of any description is a real difficulty

for her as it sometimes is for me, and I suspect for many others with more nimble fingers on occasion.
We live at a time when looks are everything and the importance of promotion is such that the package is often, perhaps not surprisingly, more expensive than the food it contains. In their quest for an eye catching product and the claimed interests of quality, manufacturers make no allowance for ageing finger joints. Double wrapped for extra freshness usually spells nightmare for arthritic digits. 'Look how big these jars are, I'll never get through all that. They don't seem to worry about people living on their own these days. The food doesn't taste the same now you know. Your Dad used to say that we're all being slowly poisoned. Heaven knows what little Scott and Faye are eating'. When I look at the long list of chemicals and other ingredients listed on the packaging of the food I buy for her I find it difficult to disagree, and the thought does occur to me that for better or worse my grandchildren will be the first generation ever to be reared from birth on chemical additives.
'I do go on don't I. I could talk till the cows come home. Put the kettle on Jim, I'm dying for another cup of strong tea'.

Sometimes when she talks about the past, I begin to appreciate just how much change this generous and often emotional lady has lived through and how much change she has seen. She remembers more gentle times when Easter was a time for rolling hard boiled eggs in Albert Park. When Christmas was a more holy feast commemorating the birth of Christ, decorations were holly trees decorated with red candles, and pork was eaten at Christmas dinner with traditional Christmas pudding all washed down with home made ginger wine. When Christmas presents were stockings filled with an apple and orange, some nuts and a new penny. If good King Wenceslas were to look down now he would see that his feast had been reduced to no more than an aggressive commercial venture devoid of the Christian message, and his doorstep carollers were sometimes less than pleased if you are slow to respond to their renditions:

If you haven't got a penny, a ha'penny will do,
If you havn't got a ha'penny,
Your door's going through....

At other times during an evening meal I am reminded of the TV programme 'Talking Heads' and I learn first hand about a long forgotten lifestyle. 'Every morning mother used to wash down the pavement in front of the house and clean the front step and the window sill.. She would polish the door brasses and letter box until they shone. Everyone in the street did it you see.

It showed they were decent and respectable folk. Then she would lock the front door and everyone would have to use the back'. I regularly hear mention of copper kettles blackened with smoke from the black leaded kitchen range, and a Kitchen blackened with layers of soot following the visit of the chimney sweep. Of fragile gas mantles and penny in the slot gas meters, washing up with soda water, the weekly bath in a metal tub in front of the fire in the kitchen on a Saturday night, and the noisy visits of the 'midden men' who came along the back arches once a week after midnight to empty the chemical closets in the brick outhouse in back yard. 'I was only a young girl then but I was the eldest and every week I was sent to collect the disinfectant from the town hall. We were all afraid of catching diphtheria at the time. My younger sisters Doris and May caught it and died. Mother was heartbroken and when I fell ill she said she would cure me herself. She wouldn't let the doctor see me until I was over the worst. She cured me with Fenwicks fever cure and hot salts in a bag around my throat. You can't beat the old fashioned remedies you know'. With half of the British population hooked on some form of therapy and the other half popping pills she still believes that a good dose of castor oil would cure most of the country's ills. 'Can you close the door Jim, there's a terrible draught round my shoulders.

She tells me of the different jobs she had as a young girl. I have heard the stories before but I listen again with a renewed interest as she goes back in time. 'Girls either went into service or worked in a shop when they left school. I left school at fourteen. We didn't have a lot of money and I had to take a part time job. I had long hair then and like the other girls I used to tie it up in a bun'. She talks of her first job in Garnett's sweet and toffee factory which was located just round the corner in Ayresome street. 'I had to dip a bowl of sweets into a big tub of melted hot chocolate but I couldn't stand the heat and I was frightened I would fall in it'. Of others in a fish and chip shop, 'I didn't like using the chipper, I had a dread of chopping a finger off', and as a nanny, 'she had me doing all sorts of housework I shouldn't be doing like cleaning the brasses. She never let me dust the fine china though'. Her final job was in a grocers shop where she met my father who was manager there. 'A gypsy woman came in one day and when I gave her a quarter of tea she told me my fortune. She said that I would never be rich, never be poor, never want for anything and I would have a long life. She also said that I would marry the manager. It all came true. Isn't that strange'. 'You've got a little bit of cream at the side of your mouth', I say, and she removes it with a delicate brush of her lace handkerchief.

I often reflect on just how much has occurred in her lifetime. She has lived through a century of remarkable change. From gas jet to Jumbo jet, from

Royal mail to E mail, from man in the moon to man on the moon, from wireless to world wide web and dolly mixtures to Dolly the sheep. She has seen the introduction of many things which we now take for granted. From zip fasteners, potato crisps and Mars Bars, to frozen food and tea bags. She can recollect local events which occurred before my own time and which my own children now regard as history.
Sometimes she is surprisingly knowledgeable. 'I saw King George the Fifth open the Transporter bridge. All the schoolchildren were given a bar of chocolate with the King's head on it. I tried to walk over the top of it afterwards with my friend Florrie but we were afraid and had to go back down. He changed the name of the Royals to Windsor and was the first King to make a Christmas broadcast on the wireless you know'. She clearly remembers when news of the sinking of the Titanic filtered through to the general public. 'People came out into the street in a state of shock. They couldn't believe such a thing could happen. It was supposed to be unsinkable. The same thing happened during the first world war when many of the young men in the street were tragically killed at the same time. It was a very tight community in those days'. She can still remember some of their names, 'his mother was never the same after the terrible news'.

She can still manage to play the piano a little. With the sound of Tchaikowsky's Nut Cracker Suite or Ivor Novello's Rustle Of Spring come the ghosts of the past, when family and friends sat around the piano in the front parlour in their Sunday best over a glass of stout. 'My mother was a good pianist and she taught me to play the piano. Families don't seem to get together any more now do they. There's no time to talk to each other any more. Some of them don't even have time to sit down together for their meals. Every one seems to be in so much of a hurry these days'. She pauses a moment and utters a little sigh. 'What have we come to'. I say, 'More importantly where are we going to'.
She is appalled at what passes for entertainment on the television now. In this matter I share her concern for a medium that has destroyed the art of conversation and reduced many children to making little more than an occasional grunt of acknowledgment. Although Britain started the world's first high definition television service in 1936, the signal was limited to London and the Home Counties. In the event, few of my mother's generation could witness the birth of a medium that would challenge radio and the written word and eventually transform the very way we live. Though it wasn't missed at that time it would certainly be missed now, but I wish I could believe that this astonishing medium has all been for the greater good. Today's programmes are not all dreadful but there too many dreadful programmes. Lord Reith must be turning in his grave at today's mindless

television with it's harsh discordant music and continuous depiction of all that is offensive, in our society. Unfortunately the shear volume of material available to the viewer from the arrival of satellite, cable and digital transmissions, together with the ensuing inevitable ratings war, have all inevitably contributed to a progressive dumbing down to an ever lower level of graphic programmes. The question now arises as to how low a level can you get.... 'There's so much rubbish on the television these days and it's all for young people', she continues, 'there's no nice music any more. Where have all the musical acts gone. Whatever happened to the old Palace Of Varieties in Corporation Road. Don't those flowers on the hall table look nice. I must remember to water them'.
The Empire as it was called then is a less prestigious bingo hall now. When I was a small boy we used to have seats booked in the orchestra stalls for the first house every Tuesday night. The next act was displayed on small boards placed on trestles on either side of the sloping dusty stage, and to the likely distress of the person behind, I can recall sitting uncomfortably on my tipped up seat up to get a better view of the short unrelated performances and the orchestra which played in the pit to accompany them. Come the interval, midway in the performance, a fire curtain came down to allow information as to where you could obtain a Hammonds organ or piano to be projected on to it. At such times I would get very restless, my mother would open a box of Clarnico chocolates and my father would retreat to the crowded bar at the back of the stalls for a pint of best Bass.
I have tuned her portable radio to classic FM so she can hear some of that nice music she often talks about, but I don't think she listens much. She enjoys the soaps on the television though and their storylines usually figure largely in conversations with older members of the family when they get together. At such times discussion invariably turns to the last war at some stage and the night some luckless German pilot dropped a bomb on the Albert Park Hotel close to where we lived. 'Dad was on fire duty that night and saw the whole thing. We were all scared out of our wits. You were asleep in next door's Anderson shelter. I remember it was always ankle deep in water. No wonder we were always full of cold. When you think of it we could have all slept safely in our beds during the entire war'.

Sometimes she gets the family photographs out to show me. She keeps them with her other mementoes in an old brown suitcase which has Dad's initials engraved on it in faded gold lettering. I recognise it from my childhood days. 'Your Dad was a good dancer you know. We used to go to all the big dances in the town hall crypt before he had his accident. He was never the same after that'. Ironically my father broke his ankle on an unlit hidden step in the Doctor's surgery of all places... The older photographs are yellowing round the edges a little now. At a time before compact cameras were readily available they all have 'Forest Wompra Grange Road' stamped on the back. In an age when a glimpse of stocking was considered more than shocking, they show ladies sitting in long voluminous dresses, high necked blouses and large feathered hats, and older gentlemen with waxed moustaches, starched white collars and sober black suits, standing upright and military like behind them. 'That's Uncle Jim. He was a big man and weighed over twenty stone but he was as gentle as a giant and that's me in my wedding dress on my wedding day. It was beautiful and warm for February but shortly afterwards the weather turned bitterly cold and your Dad caught pneumonia. It was very serious in those days and he nearly died you know. It's not as serious now though is it. They have 'antiboctics' and things. Good heavens I don't know where the time goes. Life is only short isn't it'. I tell her I know what she means and that time doesn't stop for anyone.

Many of the life threatening illnesses that plagued the first half of the last century have long since been eradicated. I have no doubt that my mother's long life and good health is due in no small measure to the advances in science, medicine and hygiene in the second half, but it is a National disgrace that so many spurious organisations receive far more consideration and often more funding than more deserving causes. Such contemptible action sadly deprives the less fortunate of those of our elderly who cannot afford quality long-term care and attention, often after devoting a lifetime of quality life time care and attention to others. Indeed a recent national survey has shown that what the public want most from our failing National Health Service is free quality care for the elderly. With the current on going loss and closure of Residential and Nursing Homes over the last decade through lack of funding and needless bureaucracy, many of our elderly and infirm are obliged to move on often to more unsuitable accommodation. Many have a speech impediment and often without family or friends they are unable to communicate any thoughts, wishes or intentions they may have. Having already lost their spouse, home, possessions and their health, many become 'bed blockers' in the trolley wards of our dirty, overcrowded and understaffed hospitals, whilst others die in the process. Surely this cannot be right.

My mother admits to having had a long and wonderful life. As for myself I have never known a life without her. 'I'm sure someone up there is looking after me', she says, 'I must have a guardian angel. I've had my share of happiness and I've nothing to reproach myself with. I've never owed a halfpenny and never let a day go by without a little prayer'.
When she does receive her telegram from the palace to mark her one

hundredth birthday - and I'm sure she will - I will have already had my allotted three score years and ten, but the chances are that she will still be concerned that her only son is looking after himself and not working too hard. 'You're only young yet Jim', she says. Nice isn't it, and long may it continue. The new millennium just wouldn't be the same without her.....

*Postscript....*

*Mam did receive her telegram from the Queen and happily celebrated her one hundredth birthday surrounded by family and friends. Sadly she passed away before publication of this book but not before she had seen and read this resume of her long life. It had a real significance for her then and I dedicate it to her memory now. Understandably the new millennium won't be the same without her....*

# 2. MORE POIGNANT OVER THE YEARS

*My father lived through only three quarters of the last century but I felt that it would be churlish of me not to indulge his memory. He was after all just another ordinary man, but he was very special to me.*

❖

The hardy Spring daffodils on the adjoining grassy mounds bent almost double in the biting Northerly wind as I as I hurried along the gravel path in the late afternoon sunshine toward the isolated Chapel of Remembrance. I had made this emotional visit many times before, but my father had passed away on this very date twenty five years ago and the occasion was somewhat special. Ten years older than my mother and born toward the end of the Victorian era, he would have been one hundred years old on this very day. His name would be displayed again in the Book of Remembrance and after a quarter of a century I wanted to indulge his memory again at this particular time.
When I quietly lifted the latch of the heavy oak door and stepped inside the small converted chapel there was nobody about. The cold stone floor of the entrance porch echoed to the sound of my solitary footsteps and the air was heavy with the scent of flowers which had been carefully arranged on opposite walls. One of the fluorescent lights directly over the display cases flickered from time to time as if to direct me to my personal goal. Time stops for no man. It came as no surprise therefore to discover that many more names of the recently departed had been added to those now familiar illuminated pages since my last visit. Many more would be added before my next.

Silence is the gratitude of true reflection. After reading the short inscription which the family had thought so long and hard over, I sat on one of the hard chapel benches, and thought back to my father's later years in the sixties when, despite the pressures of work and family, something told me I should spend more time with him. Youth lives on hope, older age on memory. 'I only drink halves now', he would say over a glass of beer in his local pub. His had been a working class upbringing. For many years he had been a member of the local Liberal Club in Corporation road where foaming drinks were routinely served in overfull pint glasses by understanding middle aged barmaids, and where he early made his name on the green baize of the snooker table. Once a betting man always a betting man.

As you would expect in such an environment neither the horses nor the dogs escaped his attention, and at a time before the organizers of Camelot made their fortunes by encouraging people who could least afford it to spend money on the lottery, he also speculated a few bob on the football pools each week. Despite his having the same numbers for years and not winning anything, he remained convinced that one day his luck would change and in a parody of a future Dell Boy would often exclaim that, 'one day we'll be millionaires'. We talked about the cricket results and the football scores, his past and my future and those days and the old days. As father and son we marvelled at the space race and worried over the Cuban missile crisis. We were equally saddened by the assassination of president Kennedy, appalled at the Vietnam war, overjoyed at winning the World cup, proud of the launching of Cunard's QE2, and amazed when man walked on the moon.

Our now familiar chat often turned toward his earlier years. 'Life was not as easy then as it is now. I had to leave school at fourteen like my older brothers and take a job in a grocery store weighing tea and sugar into little blue bags and doing other odd jobs. My family needed the money to survive. Someone came round every week to collect the rent and if you got into serious arrears the bailiffs came round and took away the furniture. I remember my mother used to pay sixpence a week so we could have the doctor call if any of my brothers was ill. There was no National Health Service to care for you in those days you know. Here put another half in that glass Jim and get one for yourself '.
I could have voiced my own thoughts on such occasions but I chose not to. In some respects after fifty odd years we seemed to have come full circle I reflected. With routine hospital and nursing home closures, a desperate shortage of doctors and nurses, a disgraceful lack of intensive care beds, long waiting times for routine operations, and talk of dirty wards and third world standards, perhaps we have not made as much progress as we should have made nor are we as caring a society as we would care to think. With recent claims that the ailing elderly are deprived of life saving equipment and left to die, sometimes in a post code lottery without clinical audit, perhaps we are not as civilised either.

Typical of his generation he used to talk about the first world war a lot. 'There's not many survivors of that pointless slaughter left now', he would say, 'most of the men in my street volunteered at the same time as me and joined one of what we called the 'Pals Battalions'. They were made up of volunteers who wanted to be kept in the same regiment. We had grown up together and some of them were only sixteen. We all thought it would be a great adventure and we would be home by Christmas'. I recalled the sepia coloured photograph which was taken shortly after he joined up and which my mother kept amongst other treasured family photographs in an old brown leather suitcase. Tall, slim and guards manlike, holding a cane at his side and proudly standing erect in his army uniform, he cut a handsome figure at the time.

For him and the rest of those idealistic young men however, events didn't turn out quite as they expected. The novelty of a smart uniform was soon eclipsed by the horrors of trench warfare. If Lord Kitchener was the inspiration then surely Douglas Haig was the planner of that first and last cruel war of attrition fought in the barren cratered landscape of the Western Front. A war in which a million men from the British Empire had their lives cut cruelly short. Mentally and physically exhausted there would be no celebrations for those who survived the carnage when the armistice was signed on the 11th hour of the 11th day of the 11th month in 1918. It was a wicked waste of a generation and for those involved in the senseless carnage it must have been a terrible ordeal. He had told the stories many times before of course, the bloody battles of Verdun, Ypres, the Somme and Passchendaele, but their retelling somehow grew more poignant over the years.

The more I listened the more I learned, and the more I learned the more I came to appreciate just what it must have been like in the front line trenches in Belgium and Northern France. The constant fatigue of the mud and the rain. The endless days and nights without food or sleep. The ravages of disease and dysentery. The horror of living in close confinement with rotting corpses and giant rats and lice, with everyday exposure to mortar shells and poison gas, all whilst facing the prospect of drowning in mud or severe maiming or death by the new machine gun when the order came to go over the top, could not possibly be imagined. 'The worst time was the winter. There was no shelter. It was so cold and you couldn't change out of your wet clothes sometimes for weeks on end. Some men froze to death and some just gave up the will to live. Some even committed suicide. I guess I was lucky to survive. You see this scar......' He had been wounded in the neck apparently. Some shrapnel from a nearby exploding shell. Whilst he was recovering behind the lines he had turned a nasty yellow colour. Not knowing the reason for this but fearing the spread of a virulent epidemic throughout the front line trenches, he was kept under close observation by a medical team in an isolation unit of a field hospital until he casually mentioned that he had been bitten by a rat whilst lying wounded in the mud. During the time of his quarantine almost all of his battalion were killed at the front including most of the men in his street......

How ironic it is I thought that the impetus for the revival of the economic growth which ended the years of depression that followed the first world war, was provided by a rearmament programme which resulted in a second.

He used to recall the misery of those depression years following the Wall Street crash in the late twenties, when it was impossible to find any work in the North. He travelled to London where he teamed up with someone selling vacuum cleaners. 'One day he just up and left with all the possessions we had'. The ladder of life is full of splinters and we gather most of them when we are sliding down. Following that escapade with little or nothing left to his name he fell ill with pneumonia after sleeping rough on the embankment. He had nothing but praise for the Salvation Army who found him. 'I would probably have died if they hadn't given me food and shelter'.
As a British nuclear test veteran, I recently had occasion to attend a Salvation Army meeting as part of a memorial service to those who had suffered and died as a result of exposure to radiation during the tests. The service was held in a bright clean modern building, but it was to the rear of this citadel that their real work was accomplished. This was where the drug addicts, drop outs, drunks and down and outs were given help and encouragement, and it was here that the depressed, impoverished, sick and disabled were offered hospitality, rest and recuperation. These are the people who could really be called carers, and these are the people who for nearly a half century have truly administered the spiritual and corporal works of mercy to the destitute. After the service I was proud to march behind their renowned brass band and familiar flag in honour of my more unfortunate colleagues. When the smiling Aunt Sally girls used to come round my local pub in their smart black and white uniforms and cute little hats with copies of the 'War Cry' in gloved hands, I always put a little something in their collection boxes in dad's memory. I know he would have wanted that. Sadly enough they don't seem to come round now as often as they did.

Sometimes he would recount the story of how he first met my mother, when as a young girl she went to work in the same small grocery store where he was employed at the time as an under manager. 'Apparently an old gypsy lady had come into the shop one day and told her that one day she would marry me. It was a big joke of course but we kept in touch and I looked her up again when I came back from London. Her father didn't like me much though. He thought I was too old for her. When I first called round to take her to the pictures he told me to go and find someone my own age. After that we got on quite well together. As you know he was a painter and decorator and he decorated our first house as a wedding present. He mixed all his own colours. You don't do that now do you'.
I can vaguely remember my grandfather. My mother used to take me round

to see him on Saturday mornings after he had finished work. I seem to recollect that he was usually still wearing his paint streaked white overalls. They had big front pockets that he kept his brushes in. He would give me my "Saturday penny" with instructions not to spend it all at once. A penny bought a lot of goodies in those days and once in the local corner sweet shop it was difficult choosing from the rows of shiny glass bottles and jars on display. Sweets or lemonade. Such a princely some would buy some of each if you had a mind to, and I usually had a mind to. Strangely enough I remember my grandfather in death rather than in life. When he died he was dressed in his best Sunday clothes and laid out in an open coffin which was placed on a table in the front parlour. Lovingly bathed and shaved, his head rested on a red velvet cushion and his grey moustache was freshly waxed. As was the custom at the time his family kept constant vigil, and all the neighbours in the street came to pay their last respects over a strong cup of tea or something a little stronger. I recall it was the first time I had seen a dead person and the experience left a profound impression on me for a long time. Hands crossed over chest, eyelids closed, an odd smile on the lips, so cold, so stiff, so still - and so final. Must have been my tender years.

On other occasions my father would recall the circumstances of my own birth in the small terraced house in Tavistock Road. In the wee small hours of one hot and humid July morning he had sat on one of the wooden benches in the little park opposite awaiting the switching on and off of the light in the front bedroom which would signal my arrival into this world. 'There was a violent thunderstorm later that day and your mother put you in the cupboard under the stairs. She did the same thing when the air raid sirens sounded during the war'. I remembered little of my own early years much beyond happily playing in that park in short trousers before my use of reason arrived. When it did the world had been plunged into another world war. Shortly afterwards my father lost his clerical job in Middlesbrough and went to work as a supervisor in a factory in the Midlands. 'Your mother didn't like the idea. It meant leaving home but we needed the money and I wanted to do something for the war effort. Everybody did at the time'.
I later discovered that the factory made tank links for the aptly named Churchill tank. Less of a factory and more of a foundry, it was dark, hot, noisy and extremely oppressive inside and his legacy of chest problems could not have been helped by the clouds of dust which fell from the sand moulds swinging on the endless conveyor belts.
My mother and I joined him complete with our pet canary after he rented a family room on the first floor over a public house which was located close to the factory. Since he was partial to a drink of beer, the advantage of living over such an establishment was not completely lost on him. Expectation

however often fails when most it promises. Living in one room and sharing a less than clean kitchen, bathroom and toilet with two other families and the landlord's household, was not an easy matter. I recall the cramped conditions and the complete lack of privacy but any complaints about standards of hygiene, cleanliness or other privations were usually met with the rejoinder that 'There is a war on you know'.
When a large dog from the adjoining flat stole into our room one day and made off with a freshly roasted joint which had been cooked as a special treat on Dad's birthday, and which had been obtained after saving many weeks of precious meat coupons, she decided that it was time to return home - with or without the canary.

My father put on a bit of weight after the war years when he resumed his clerical occupation. It could have been his genes but it was more likely due to a combination of my mother's home cooking, his fondness for a glass of beer or two - or three - with the lads after work and, like most of his generation, a complete lack of exercise. Ever clothes conscious in an age before the leisure clothes industry changed the dress code from formal to informality, I never saw him in anything other than a dark suit and shirt, starched studded collar with tie and black shoes. Certainly a party to the 'If you want to get ahead get a hat' brigade, he always wore one to work, even in the cloying heat of a Summer's day. Schooled at a time when the great majority of families could afford only one set of working clothes and another as Sunday best, he would be both surprised and offended at the demeaning casual jeans and denim jackets, baggy trousers and sweatshirts and the trainers and back to front baseball caps of today's more casual dress code. They would be as unwelcome on his voyage through life as would the new brash and violent code of conduct they have generally come to epitomise.

His weight cannot have helped him in late middle age when tragedy struck and he fell awkwardly over an unlit step, ironically enough in the doctor's surgery. 'I looked down and saw my foot was pointing in the wrong direction'. There followed a number of operations to reset it correctly but it proved to be a setback from which he never fully recovered. 'I could have claimed compensation but the doctor, who I knew quite well, told me he wasn't insured. He gave me a couple of hundred quid as I remember but I should have settled for a lot more'. In the ever increasing claims conscious society of today, reinforced as it is by a raft of European directives on human rights and the 'no win, no fee' mentality of the legal profession, he could have claimed thousands.
In later life he suffered a heart attack and had to settle for a pill popping less active life. When he developed the inevitable chest problems and breathing

difficulties the burden of looking after him fell to my mother. As was often required of the first born daughter at the time, she had spent much of her early life looking after her younger brothers and sisters when her mother died. Now life had come full circle for her. Once again she was required to don the mantle of carer.

Youth is a blunder, manhood a struggle and older age often a regret. I was glad that I spent those final years with him, but at the same time saddened that I had not spent more time with him when I was younger and valued his company more when I was older. Like all of those of his generation who made the same sacrifice, and many of those who made the ultimate sacrifice, he held the same values through two world wars and was determined to do the best for his family. He had no grand estate or financial riches to pass on, but looking back over the years, I never really wanted for anything and he was always there when there was anything I wanted. His society had it's problems and his generation was not perfect, but amongst other attributes care of the sick and the elderly was enshrined in family life. I fear the likes of his generation with it's respect for family life will not be seen again in our new materialistic world of instant gratification. His was far removed from the so called caring society of today which boasts the worst record in Western Europe for care of children and the elderly, where more than one in three marriages ends in divorce and ten per cent of homes are run by a lone parent. Things never stay the same I mused. They can only get better or worse. Shuffling about now on that hard bench seat I came to the conclusion that it is a brave man indeed to conclude that they can only get better.

The noise of the chapel door opening intruded on my reverie. 'We're closing now', an officious looking attendant announced.
After my recollections of more poignant years, the manner of his curt announcement disturbed me somewhat, but I reasoned that his was only a job. A short while later and I was making my way back to the car park in the still blustery wind. It is at such times that the mind is filled with images of one's own mortality, and I pondered on the likelihood of my own son and daughter making their way along this very path at some more distant time to make the same pilgrimage for me. It was a sobering thought.

# 3. A FAMILIAR PARK BENCH

*We cannot choose the time of our arrival into this world nor can we choose the place. Like all those of my generation my formative years were largely conditioned by the second world war. Old enough to reason about but too young to participate in, those years of austerity and their aftermath are but a distant memory now but they were real enough at the time.*

❖

I had not anticipated arriving so early for a meeting with some of my friends that evening so I strolled to the nearby park and sat on a familiar looking wooden bench. My father had probably sat on one similar more than half a century ago awaiting my arrival into this world. It had apparently long been decided that if their offspring were a boy he would be called James. Since my father was a well built man in later life it was inevitable that we would be forever referred to as big and little Jim.

Youth lives on hope, older age on memories. Sitting there after all those years in the warm early evening sunshine, it was inevitable that the memories would come flooding back. Not those of innocent early childhood before the use of reason, when toddlers discover that inviting looking snow melts and hands can get cold and wet despite two layers of gloves, that the rims of wellington boots can chafe the backs of legs and make them sore, and that sometimes it's better to be inside looking out than outside looking in. Neither those of learning that kittens can scratch and puppies can bite and falls can result in painful cuts and bruises, and it was normal to be afflicted with scarlet fever, whooping cough, the mumps, chicken pox, the measles and other such ailments shortly after starting school. Nor were they recollections of Hornby railways, Dinky Toys and Meccano, of ludo, snakes and ladders and tiddly winks, of car numbers and train spotting, of making kites and playing conkers or marbles when 'blood eyes' and steel 'bongos' were a prized possession in an age of make believe when imagination made up for what wasn't available. Such memories had been lost in the mists of time. These were more clouded images of growing up in times of hostility. Unlike the declaration of the first world war only twenty five years previously, few believed that hostilities would be over by Christmas when Prime Minister Neville Chamberlain announced the beginning of the second armed conflict on that fateful September morning.

Early in the struggle I was evacuated to a signalman's cottage adjoining a small railway station in the country near Kirkbymoorside, but unfortunately what this retreat boasted in rural charm it lacked in basic urban amenities. To a young boy such things are of little consequence. Any hopes I may have cherished of an idyllic wartime of long warm Summers playing in fields of long grass, climbing trees or watching trains go by from an LNER signal box, were quickly dashed. In the phoney war before the arrival of the Luftwaffe gave some fact to H.G. Well's fiction in 'The Shape Of Things To Come', my mother decided that it would be better if her only son were to return home. When I did return I found that the metal railings which surrounded the little park in front of our house had been removed to make battle tanks, one next door neighbour had surprisingly sunk an Anderson air raid shelter into their much prized rose garden, and the other had installed a Morrison table shelter in the front room. A barrage balloon had been sited on a nearby allotment, but despite frequent excited visits I never did see it in the air. One windy day it broke loose from it's mooring cables and shortly afterwards caught fire during an electrical thunderstorm. 'Came down just like the R101', a neighbour said. In one corner of the park opposite a public air raid shelter was in the course of construction. It had a gently sloping entrances at opposite corners which led down to a warren of concrete tunnels lined each side with crude canvas bunks. When we first had occasion to use it, one cold winters night after the sound of the wailing air raid sirens had urged us from our warm beds, we discovered that the floor of the shelter was covered with muddy water to the depth of the lower bunks. Not surprisingly the shelter fell into disuse early in the war, but with the innocence of boyhood, I can remember wondering what young couples could possibly be doing when they furtively disappeared into the blackness of the interior for a half hour or so.
With the advent of the darker nights we carried torches when we ventured outside after dark. Ever fearful of aerial bombardment all the windows of the houses in the road were criss-crossed with sticky tape and provided with black out curtains, and the headlights of vehicles were masked to the extent that I wondered how any light at all could possibly shine through them. In the all consuming darkness 'Put that light out', became a familiar cry of the more alert fire wardens.

Early in the war sweets and chocolate disappeared from the shops for the duration. Ironically enough when it was no longer possible to buy pontefract cakes, sherbert fountains, dolly mixtures, blackjacks and sticks of liquorice, children's teeth proved to be the healthiest on record. With the later essential rationing of all meat and dairy products on the home front and the consumption of locally grown fruit and vegetables after a 'Dig for Victory'

campaign, many would claim that the nation's diet during the war years was one of the most healthiest on record. Certainly my generation appeared to thrive on it, and strangely enough among other things, I retain a long held fondness for dried egg from those times of austerity.
To my dismay the cinemas in keeping with other places of public entertainment closed in the interests of public safety, but shortly afterwards to my delight they opened again in the interests of public morale. Like all families hungry for news we regularly gathered around the wireless set to listen to news bulletins on the BBC and I recalled the occasional events which lifted the gloom during those dark days. When Bruce Belfrage gave the nation the news of the successful evacuation of our army from the beaches at Dunkirk, the next door neighbours came in for a celebratory drink, and in the spirit of the camaraderie which was abroad they invited us into their shelter next time there was an air raid. 'It's nice and dry and we have a paraffin heater but it's best to bring a couple of blankets and a nice flask of hot tea'. As an impressionable youngster, I had thrilled to the Pathe News coverage of the Battle of Britain, and I recalled that the sinking of the Bismark prompted the ringing of church bells for the first time since the beginning of the war. Their chimes before then would have signalled an invasion.
It was about this time that a lone German aircraft dropped the bomb which demolished the Albert Park Hotel. Not as strategic a target as the Bismark perhaps. There would be no bell ringing in Germany to celebrate the event, but it was my father's local pub which was noted for the quality of it's draught bass and he never forgave that unknown German pilot for his indiscretion. Thankfully no one was hurt and for my part it gave me the first opportunity to collect some much prized shrapnel. 'Sure that's not part of a beer pump....' but I was adamant.
Entertainment like household coal was in short supply. I recalled the long winter nights crouched round the glowing coals of a single fire in the sitting room listening to Sandy McPherson, The Bandwagon Show or Monday Night At Eight-o-Clock, 'oh can't you hear the chimes....', on our bakelite wireless set before the bedtime drink of Ovaltine. Despite the warmth of the evening I involuntarily shuddered at the thought of retiring to those cold comfort bedrooms where the very breath hung in the icy air as I climbed between the equally cold sheets.

When my father lost his job in Middlesbrough he found another one in a munitions factory in the Midlands. It meant his leaving home to work in Leamington spa, but our separation did not last too long after he found a family room we could rent on the first floor of a Public House. An advantage not entirely lost on him.

The long wartime journey to our new abode one short Winter's day was not without incident. My fascination with steam trains and everything about them, served to take my mind off the treasured bicycle that I had left behind and the daunting prospect of starting a new school. 'You can take the ludo board and the snakes and ladders but nothing else'. No comfort of Inter City Services to speed you direct to your destination then. No reserved seat by the window in a warm carriage or the luxury of a trolley service to provide you with a refreshing drink. The dimly lit unheated compartments were filled to capacity with men and women of all ages and all ranks of the armed services, their heavy kitbags and other equipment barely contained by the overhead storage racks. Many more were packed into the smoke filled corridors which were almost impossible to negotiate. In the absence of anything to do there was little or nothing to see out of the dirt streaked windows where condensation ran down in little rivulets. With the engine's fire box a sure giveaway to the enemy at night, the train would sometimes have to stop outside a town or city before being cleared to enter the station. Amusingly enough it was at such times that our pet canary, which at the last moment we had decided to bring with us in it's covered cage, would often start to sing....

To an impressionable young boy the hustle and the bustle of the blackened out and unidentified steam wreathed stations were a hive of fascinating activity. The reality of those war times however could be found in the crowded waiting rooms where, in addition to those declaring that 'Spitting is forbidden', asking 'Is your journey really necessary', urging us to 'Dig for victory' and telling us that 'We should spend less on ourselves and more on National savings', there were others reminding us to 'Make way for the guns', for the railways were 'The lines behind the lines'. On a more ominous note there were others depicting mock caricatures of Hitler and Goering as our fellow travellers informing us that there were spies everywhere and 'Careless talk costs lives'.

Living as a family in one room over a pub at that time was not easy. There was little or no privacy. With beds in opposite corners and a small table with a couple of chairs in the centre, there was space for little else except the canary, which seemingly oblivious to the smell of stale beer and other privations continued to sing throughout the entire war. We shared a kitchen, bathroom and toilet with two other tenants who had large dogs, and the landlord's family who had a fondness for cats. Under such trying circumstances it must have been particularly difficult for my mother who did what she could to keep the place clean and tidy, but any complaints about cold water, the state of the weekly wash, food hygiene or other shortcomings were usually met with the rejoinder that 'There is a war on you know'.

Shortly after our move the Germans raided the industrial city of Coventry only a few miles to the North. They called the operation 'Moonlight Sonata'. The city was the target of a massive air raid which killed over five hundred people and destroyed sixty thousand buildings in the city centre. Unprecedented numbers at a time before Bomber Harris reaped his whirlwind revenge over Hamburg, Dresden, Berlin.... I recalled the familiar unsynchronised drone of the enemy aircraft as they flew overhead guided by the light of the gathering inferno, the play of the searchlights on the underside of the broken cloud, the dull thud of distant explosions, the distant flickering light and the pall of black smoke in the late Autumn sky which bore testament to the many fires which raged unabated for two days. Thankfully it was the nearest we came to the blitz, but such was the resolve of the inhabitants that when we were able to visit that brave city a week or two later, we discovered that the buses were running again between the rubble, the dog track had reopened and, to our disappointment, 'House Full' notices had been posted at the Hippodrome theatre.

Against the wavering fortunes of the combatants in a now global war I recalled my simple boyhood pursuits. To a ten year old, the surprising invasion of Russia and the infamous attack by the Japanese on Pearl Harbour, were far less important than making dens and climbing trees, swimming in the River Leam and hitching lifts on the colourful barges which operated on the local canal, or train spotting at the main line station where London Paddington or Bristol Temple Meads sounded far more exciting places. Oblivious to a world in turmoil I learned the more mischievous arts of making a catapult and scrumping apples from local orchards on the way home from school. Then there were the interesting situations at the local places of interest. I smiled at their recollection but they were certainly considered serious at the time. Warwick, where much to my mother's horror one Summer I suddenly plunged into the River Avon to swim to the other side and back. Kenilworth, where I got lost in the castle maze, and Stratford, where my father, who was a heavy man who had little experience in small boats and no experience in rowing them, came close to capsizing the frail craft which we had hired.
Sometimes of a late Sunday morning after church service, I would take a flask of hot soup and sandwiches to my father at his place of work where his duties were that of supervisor. On one occasion he took me inside one of the simple steel sheeted buildings which made up the factory complex. Not knowing quite what to expect I recoiled at the darkness, the oppressive cloying heat and the harsh discordant noise which made conversation almost impossible. In this harsh environment the perspiring Irish work force carried out their routine tasks wearing goggles, face masks and aprons to

protect them from the searing heat of the open furnaces and the swirling dust which covered anything and everything. All in all I was more glad to come out than I was to go in.

With the on going ebb and flow of battle in North Africa, much talk among adults about fifty thousand GI brides and retaliatory one thousand bomber raids over Germany, our plug-in wireless set continued to provide the main source of news and entertainment. 'The Brains Trust' with professor Joad, or 'Twenty Questions' with Anona Winn, may have been popular with the older generation, but other programmes like 'ITMA' had more appeal to youngsters, 'Can I do you now Sir....' A visit to the pictures was a must once a week but you could never walk straight in. 'You go and stand in the queue and dad and I will join you as soon as we can'.
Leisure and entertainment was limited in those trying times but boyhood soon finds it's own outlets. Whilst my parents might be visiting the elegant Regency style 'Pump Rooms' where, despite food rationing, it was still possible to indulge in traditional afternoon tea and biscuits, I took up the more adventurous pursuit of exploring the long neglected local spinney with my pals. It was however not the sort of pastime my mother approved of and, to her horror, the accident that she continuously forecast occurred when, during some energetic children's war game, I badly tore the back of my arm on some rusty barbed wire, and was rushed to hospital after losing a truly alarming amount of blood. I recalled the scar that I still carried from those far off days and, involuntarily rolling up my sleeve, I checked that it was still there.

Those who travel best know when to return. Around the time that the Allied leaders met again in Teheran to discuss he progress of the current war and make plans for the future peace, our cramped living conditions and lack of privacy were proving to be altogether too much to cope with. Tensions were running high and patience was running out. It was deemed time for my mother and I to return home with the canary and, in the year that saw the costly but successful Allied landings on the beaches of Normandy, my mother took a part time job in Newhouses Department Store and, courtesy of Rab Butler's Education act, I acquired my first school uniform and brown leather satchel to re-commence my schooling at the local Marist College.
It was here that I sat at my own desk with a lid and a hole in the top for an inkwell, in a large classroom which had cast iron radiators and a blackboard with a little ledge for the chalk and a blackboard duster that was always falling off. It was here that I first drank warm school milk from tiny bottles through a straw at mid morning and mid afternoon, and it was here that I

was first introduced to school dinners with their generous helpings of lukewarm brown windsor soup and gristly meat with two watery overcooked vegetables. We ate steamed fish on Fridays and rice pudding or semolina on most other days, all consumed in a makeshift dining hall which invariably smelt of boiled cabbage. It was here that I discovered that outside toilets reeked in the Summer and froze up in the Winter, and the Marist fathers were equally inclined toward religion and administering punishment. Surprisingly enough, the deeply held religious convictions of the Society Of Mary included the belief that to spare the rod was to spoil the child, and caning was liberally dispensed by the teacher in the classroom, the punishment master in the corridor, and the headmaster in his office. Few boys escaped the stern regime and I suspect that few parents were aware of such stern treatment. Even more surprisingly, I discovered many years later, that the nuns held the same harsh convictions and metered out an equal lack of clemency to the girls in their charge at Convent schools.

Every week marks from two to five were awarded to each and every boy for each and every subject, and on Friday mornings a black robed cane wielding headmaster brought round the dreaded black book in which they were recorded. A five was excellent and a two spelled disaster. A three would involve the cane and a two detention on a Saturday morning in addition. If you were lucky you would have a sufficient number of fives to cancel out all the threes. Life was often hard, sometimes scary, and frequently painful at St Mary's College, and I recall some particularly sore hands and frustrating Saturday mornings from those formative years.

How different from the primary schools of today, where the teaching of literacy and numeracy has been put on the back burner and twenty five per cent of eleven year olds leave unable to read or write properly. How different from the crisis in many of our inner city comprehensive schools where, in a complete role reversal, teachers go in dread of their pupils, truancy is commonplace, and examination results have to be manipulated to disguise their declining academic standards. As politics infringes more and more on the school curriculum, education in the arts and sciences is replaced with training on social studies and instructions on political correctness. The three R's have never been more neglected. Deprivation is one thing but unreasonable behaviour in our schools is another. Perhaps a return to more traditional teaching methods and a measure of the same treatment would help to bring a little order and correction into the lives of the more outrageous young teenagers who attend them. Unfortunately such old fashioned disciplines would not be tolerated now of course. I can already hear the cries of dismay and dissent from the ever growing host of social reformers and misguided politically correct advisers, but I have to say that, as unpleasant as it was at the time, the more sterner regime of my own schooldays has certainly done me no harm in later life.

Young boys soon lift their spirits. If Friday mornings were filled with apprehension, then Friday afternoons brought a new sense of purpose. The college was divided into four houses after the patron saints of George, Andrew, Patrick and David, and the competition between their respective football teams was fierce. It was a time before the words 'junk food' and 'couch potato' could be found in the English dictionary, and fish and chips were more popular than pizza, chicken masala or chow mien. A time before there were worrying statistics about overweight youngsters and British schoolchildren had given up eating fruit and vegetables, given way to eating chips with everything, and had the fastest growing rate of obesity in Europe. A time before Government began to sell off school playing fields for inconsiderate profit, and then naively wonder why there is a decline in competitive sport and we do so badly in international competitions. It was also a time before the luxury of on-field changing facilities when we thought little of walking miles from school in our heavy ill fitting football boots, to play with an even heavier laced up football on a remote soggy field of dreams - before walking back again. Notwithstanding such hardship, come rain or come shine, Friday afternoon was a time to look forward to. The homework could wait. For those who were not to be detained the following morning, the weekend started here.
There were other distractions during those early college years. When V1 doodle bugs and V2 rockets began to rain down on London and the Home Counties in a surprise second blitz bringing the possibility of them raining down on the rest of the country, precautionary air raid drills were re-introduced. At such times we all took to the cellars under the rectory where we sat on uncomfortable wooden benches in semi darkness and made faces at one another before the visors of our gas masks misted up. Despite such trials however, they often provided a welcome interruption to a difficult and potentially painful maths or Latin class.

With the overrun of the launch pads and the end of the war in sight, it was a time for boosting morale and looking to the future. If the characters in such films as 'This Happy Breed', 'The Way Ahead', 'In Which We Serve' and 'The White Cliffs Of Dover' were ordinary folk who the public could readily identify with, the moral was obvious. If they could smile through adversity and reshape their lives then so could we. If the newsreels on the course of the war provided more allegation than fact, it was inevitable that they also served to glamorise it for many young boys in their early teens and, naive to the reality, aerial warfare held a particular fascination for them. I recall animated discussion on the merits of the American Flying Fortress and the

English Lancaster bomber, both of which had done so much to bring hostilities in Europe to an end after knocking most of it down.

Strangely enough my main recollection of the end of the war in Europe is one of Winston Churchill standing on the balcony of Buckingham Palacelooking down on a vast throng of wildly celebrating people. 'We shall allow ourselves a brief moment of rejoicing....' Britain's greatest hero was stood between the King and the Queen, 'an unprecedented physical placement', the commentator said at the time. We did our own rejoicing at a street party on VE day when we did our own unprecedented physical placement of tables and chairs in the middle of the road and everyone wore party hats, ate egg and cress and fish paste sandwiches, drank home made lemonade, and danced around to gramophone records. Afterwards, when it got dark, the more adventurous lit a celebration bonfire which burnt a large hole in the tarmac. Much to my delight the whole thing was repeated a few months later on VJ day when we burnt an even larger hole, but nobody seemed to mind much.

My recollection of war years, which had both dominated my childhood and those of an entire generation, was disturbed when a group of excitable young boys wearing their favourite club's replica kit came to play a noisy game of football on the same grassed area where that public air raid shelter had been sited all those years ago. Their arrival in smart new sports wear set me thinking. Whatever happened to the short trousers which all young boys used to wear until around the time their voices broke, the vests to keep their backs warm, and the elbow patched jackets which used to serve so well as goal posts I wondered. Those frugal but halcyon days of youth were all long gone now in a world of contrived change and instant gratification for young and old alike. So many changes had occurred since those times of austerity and 'make do and mend', when, like all young boys at the time, I was often obliged to mend my own ways.
Suddenly, aware of the lengthening shadows, I checked my watch to discover that my reminiscences had made me late for my meeting. How ironic I thought that past events should have overtaken those of the future. So what I mused, there is often more to life than increasing it's speed....

# 4. THEY DON'T MAKE THEM LIKE THAT ANYMORE

*Nothing is made as it was before and this maxim is particularly true of the film world. In 1895 when the Lumiere brothers first projected a film of an oncoming train arriving at a station some of the paying audience fled in terror. They believed it was going to come out of the screen and run them over. In 1995 the first feature film using computer generated frames was made. A hundred years of cinema progress. It's history is recorded between these two landmark events and I believe my generation has been fortunate enough to enjoy the best of it.*

❖

The golden age of the cinema they called it. The forties and the fifties of the last century. When colour film finally usurped monochrome and the old black and white presentations, and brought a new sense of realism to the screen for the traditional family audience on both sides of the Atlantic. A time when such film makers as John Ford, Howard Hawks, Frank Capra and Alfred Hitchcock exploited the emerging new technology. A time when names like Twentieth century Fox, Warner brothers, United Artistes, Ealing Studios. Boulting Brothers and J. Arthur Rank, were synonymous with a world of glamour, make believe, heroism and adventure, and made some of the finest films ever made.

We didn't call them cinemas in those days though. Many were converted opera houses and variety halls, with neo-classical facades, coloured glass canopies and domed roofs, but they had re-emerged with magic names to suit the new electronic age. The Elite and Grand Electric, The Carlton and the Ritz, The Alhambra and the Regal, The Scala and The Mayfair, they all offered the public a certain glamour and a relief from the hardship and austerity of the war and it's aftermath. They also offered the technology of steriographic sound, of technicolour, cinerama, cinemascope and 3D. Unfortunately the latter required the audience to wear spectacles and the novelty soon wore off.

Unlike many of today's fallen idols, the equally glamorous film stars of the time who regularly appeared in the 'Picturegoer', 'Picture show', 'Film Pictorial' and other popular film magazines, could do no public wrong in those earlier years. The image of such stars as Humphrey Bogart and Joan Crawford, Henry Fonda and Bette Davis, James Stewart and Judie Garland, Rock Hudson and Doris Day, was carefully nurtured in the Hollywood dream factory which produced them. They were placed on a pedestal by an adoring public who looked upon them as both role models and icons. But many had feet of clay. The film stars of the time often had guilty secrets and the film studios they were contracted to did everything possible to safeguard their reputations. There often turbulent private lives, unsullied by adverse publicity and protected from the gaze of their legions of fans, remained a romantic mystery.

It was a time when it was still considered patriotic for the audience to stand for the national Anthem, which was always played at the beginning and end of each performance, and a time before a furtive few sidled out before it was finished. A time before the intrusive television set invaded our homes and took over our lives and changed them forever. Since there were few other places of public entertainment, going to the pictures at least once and sometimes twice a week became a national habit for the average family. It was an escape from reality into a world of fantasy and comedy, scares and thrills, romance and adventure.
Irrespective of what was showing it was considered a night out, and unless it was a very poor film indeed you could never expect to walk straight in. Such was their popularity that I would regularly stand in long snaking queues with my mother and father sheltering from the rain under a brolly, or stamping feet and rubbing hands on a cold winter's evening. Often there would be no real guarantee that we would gain admission or that once inside we would even be sat together. Neither was there a guarantee of a reasonable seat after the long wait. I recall that the Elite cinema in Linthorpe Road had a circular auditorium. If you were unfortunate enough to be allocated a seat in the orchestra stalls to one side and close to the screen, it was difficult to follow the vertical action which took place on it directly overhead. At some cinemas however there were compensating factors in the Summer months. Since air conditioning was a luxury in those more lean times, those of no particular intent and passing the entrance on a hot afternoon, might be enticed inside to see the matinee performance with the promise that, 'It's cooler inside'.

In my early teenage years, adamant that I had completed my homework, I recall going to the pictures with my mother and father on a Monday evening after tea.
'You two go and stand in the queue at the Gaumont for the one and three's, and I'll follow on when I've washed up and changed', my mother would say after she had cleared the tea table'.
Unless it was a very poor film indeed you could never expect to walk straight in at that time. Sometimes the head of our queue would merge with that for

the cheaper seats in the ninepenny's. As we neared the entrance with it's single ticket office, there would be loud complaints as people tried to jump from one queue to the other in desperation to see the last complete performance.
'Two at one and three, and a single at ninepence'.
The appearance of the costumed doorman was always a welcome sight after the long wait, particularly when all the spangles and fruit gums which had been bought to eat inside had been consumed in desperation, and the latest edition of the Beano and the Dandy had been read twice over.
'You go in and I'll see you inside. No need for all of us to miss part of the film. Stand up at the interval when the lights go up so I can see where you are. Maybe we can get some seats together then'.
Children could not be admitted to see films carrying an X certificate but for others they were allowed admission if they were accompanied by an adult. I recall that like most schoolboys I wore a school cap in those days and if we were watching a particularly scary film like 'The Hound Of The Baskervilles', I would hide behind it during the more frightening scenes. 'It's not real you know. It's only a film', my Dad would say. Conversely, in an effort to show how grown up I was, I would use the same cap to screen any watery eyes during such emotional films as 'Lassie Come Home', at a time when most of the audience were dabbing their own or weeping profusely into their handkerchief.
The larger more prestigious front entrance with it's entrance steps and canopy, was reserved for the one nines and the exclusive balcony seats,perhaps not surprisingly largely the preserve of the emerging younger generation. The pictures was one of the few places to take your girlfriend during the week, and many of the couples in this queue would have met for the first time at the local dance hall on the previous Saturday night, hoping to extend their familiarity in the privacy of the back row.

Cinemas were closed on Sundays. This day was still regarded as a Christian holiday and a day of worship. A day of rest and abstinence when it was considered more correct to attend church than a place of entertainment. Later they opened of an evening when there were three complete continuous performances a day for the rest of the week. Once inside, it was possible to see the matinee in the afternoon and sit through the whole of the first evening performance again if you had a mind to. If you happened to gain admission in the middle of the main or supporting film, you could see the first half before leaving. Such situations did little for the plot but the audience was rarely disappointed. Cocooned in the all concealing darkness of the smoke wreathed and cheap scented auditorium, any lack of quality in the programme was more than compensated for by quantity. In addition to the main A film there was usually a second or B film which was invariably as good and sometimes better. British Movietone news would provide an update on world events and to wet the appetite All Next Week would provide a foretaste of what was due to be shown the following week. Invariably a cry of delight from the audience would herald the showing of a Walt Disney cartoon and sometimes there would be an Edgar Lustgarten mystery to enjoy. There was also the advertisements of course informing the audience that sweets, chocolates, cigarettes and Eldorado ice cream, which was available in little cardboard tubs and eaten with a small wooden spatula, were all available in the foyer. If you were fortunate enough, as if by magic, an organist would rise from the old orchestra pit between performances to play popular music of the time.

The younger generation were not forgotten. They had their own films and cartoons to enjoy, and they enjoyed them in their own way in the manner that unsupervised children do.
On Saturday mornings many of these same stately buildings would play host to the Saturday Morning Film Club, when hundreds of excited children would run amok, stand on the seats, or run up and down the aisles before and after the performance - and sometimes during it. It was impossible to hear any of the dialogue due to the shrieking and the shouting which accompanied it, and often difficult to follow the plot in the mayhem of sweet wrappers and popcorn that was being thrown about. There was always a great deal of audience participation, and I recall with some affection, the cheers for the hero, the boo's for the villains, and the loud groans and whistles from the boys at any suggestion of any action of a romantic nature. A pantomime on film with no one to answer back, it was all very chaotic. I fear that many a cap and gloves, and even the odd coat or two would have gone missing in the mayhem. It must have been a nightmare for the cinema manager who had to keep a semblance of order during the show - and arrange for clearing up afterwards.

Despite it's status as a source of entertainment, cinema was also recognised as an art form. On one particularly memorable morning during my schooldays after morning assembly, I recall walking in company with the entire school in orderly lines of three across town, to see Shakespeare's Henry V which was showing at the new Odeon cinema in Corporation Road. The film was presumably considered worthy of viewing because of it's stirring portrayal of Shakespeare on screen, and I suspect that most schoolchildren up and down the country were allowed to see the film during school hours, in the firm belief that they would be moved by the heroic poetry and Laurence Olivier's moving portrayal of the Sovereign. Unfortunately, like most other schoolboys at the time, weaned as they were on epic British war films showing dog fights in the air, submarine warfare, POW escapes and espionage behind enemy lines, all produced and directed by filmmakers who seemed determined to show how we were winning the war, I suspect that the verse served only as a prelude to the thrilling battle scenes of Agincourt which followed it. The likes of John Mills, Richard Attenborough, Jack Hawkins and Anthony Steel have a lot to answer for.

A weekly visit to the Odeon in Stockton High Street became a regular occurrence for June and I, when an Aunt of hers who worked there at the time, handed on the two free passes which as an employee of the Rank Organisation she was entitled to. It seemed like a great privilege at the time, and needless to say, we did not hesitate to take advantage of her kind offer. Sometimes we would have a meal before the last house in the art decor cinema restaurant with it's deep plush carpet. With one eye on the time to ensure that we could take our seats before the last house commences, we would sit at tables covered with starched white tablecloths and stiffly folded dinner napkins, to eat a modest fish and chip tea with the carved heavy stainless steel cutlery. At a time before Mc Donalds, Burger King and Kentucky Fried Chicken had cornered the convenience food market, and their familiar garish outlets had appeared on every town and city high street, and eating out was not as popular as it is today, it all seemed so grand and so correct. The perfect prelude to whatever was later on offer, whether it be Thrillers - 'Vertigo', Epics - 'Ben Hur', Musicals - 'Gigi', Westerns - 'Shane', Love Stories - 'A Place In The Sun' or sometimes just shear escapism - 'Around The World In Eighty Days'. We have most of the films of that era on video now. When we watch them again, we remember our lost youth. When they are shown on national television, they are reminders of a lost age of innocence. 'Play it again Sam....'

By contrast it was in the late fifties during my National Service that I saw my first film in an open air cinema. It was the time of the British nuclear testing programme, and I had been posted with an Engineering Regiment to a remote coral Island in the Pacific where the tests were taking place. An area of sand had been raised to form a curved viewing area and the appreciative audience sat on wooden planking. Programmes started each evening at eight o'clock after dark, and such was the demand that they were changed four times a week. Under the circumstances, there was a careful avoidance of films that might carry a sexual overtone, though I can recall the scantily costume-clad Glynis Johns in 'Encore' getting a few wolf whistles. Errol Flynn capturing Burma single-handed produced some caustic comments, and the arrival of John Wayne with the cavalry in Westerns was always loudly cheered. Science fiction proved to be popular. I recall that 'The Incredible Shrinking Man' and 'The Amazing Colossal Woman', played to packed houses. Unfortunately the orientation of the cinema left much to be desired. On occasions a large bright moon would rise behind the screen midway through the performance, and on a breezy evening the screen would take on a ripple motion giving the effect of double vision. In that part of the world there were few occasions when a performance would be rained off, but there was the odd power failure to interrupt proceedings. Despite the limitations however, it became a place to escape into a world of make believe and a place to forget the harsh reality of the surroundings.

The end of the fifties also saw the last of the lavish film sets and the end of many of the studios that created them. Those that remained turned to making low budget fodder for the newly arrived all consuming television which had arrived to challenge their popularity. The rules about what you could and could not show on the cinema screen evaporated with the arrival of the promiscuous swinging sixties. The mood and taste of the nation changed, and so did it's values.
Unhappily, many of the grand old buildings which housed so many fond memories for my generation have long since been demolished, and the grandeur of many others has been sadly demeaned in their conversion into indulgent bingo halls and night clubs. By virtue of their listed building status as art decor, only the Odeon cinemas remain today as a testament to those more romantic times. Sadly, yesteryear's picture palaces have now been replaced by more impersonal multi-screened complexes, showing ever more violent and sleazy images of today's real world to the sound of an audience eating popcorn. Despite the snap and crackle and the challenge of home videos, satellite TV and DVD's, the cinema seems to be making a comeback, but few modern films seem to stir the same feelings and emotions as those shown on the silver screen of yesteryear. If the early innocent enchantment of the films of that former golden age is lost on the younger generation of our brave new world, then many of my own generation might simply say that, 'They don't make them like that anymore'.

# 5. CAN I HAVE THIS DANCE PLEASE

*The character in this story could well be me. The plot is fiction but the setting is fact. In the fifties and early sixties the social calendar for many teenagers centred round the dance hall. For some it was the centre of the universe on a Saturday night, and for others the focus of attention for most nights of the week. It was a venue to escape to and an occasion to dress up for. A time and a place where boy met girl in a more innocent world before the arrival of the flesh and the devil.*

❖

It felt strange to be standing in that room again after all those years. A curious mixture of nostalgia and lost innocence. The practice that he worked for had been commissioned to make an initial survey of the premises to determine the feasibility of an extension, and he had welcomed the opportunity to revisit this most memorable of his teenage haunts. In the late fifties, like so many of his generation before television made it's final breakthrough, he had spent many a memorable Saturday night here after an afternoon of leisure playing football and a week of serious study.
It had been the era of the big band, the 78 vinyl record, and the time when the dance hall was a mecca for teenagers who danced to Rosemary Cloony's 'This Old House', Guy Mitchell's 'Singin The Blues', and Frankie Laine's 'I Believe'. A time when Elvis Presley stormed the charts and we jived to 'Jailhouse Rock' and 'rocked around the clock' with Bill Haley's comets. A time when Cliff Richard had his first hit, and rock and roll changed teenage attitudes and hairstyles and even the way we dressed. The music was a celebration of Glen Miller and Harry James, Artie Shaw and Bennie Goodman. When Joe Loss played at the Tower ballroom in Blackpool in the Summer months, Ted Heath and his orchestra with Denis Lotis, Lita Roza and Dickie Valentine were resident at the Winter Gardens during the illumunations and Lou Praeger appeared regularly at London's Hammersmith Palais.

Enthusiasts came from all over the country to dance to the popular music of the time. At some point in the evening they would usually gather tight knit round the stage to get closer to their particular idols, to see them perform on the clarinet or the saxaphone, trumpet, piano or drums, or to simply enjoy the big band sound. Some came to enjoy the dancing and others in the hope of winning a spot prize. Some came to practise their dance steps for a future competition. They arrived early in the evening to take advantage of a deserted dance floor, and very often left before the landlord of the local pub down the road called last orders. Most came to socialise after last orders, for this was the place where boy met girl before two years of National Service claimed the remaining two years of their youth. Eyes across a crowded room one girl in particular had taken his fancy in this very place one Christmas Eve all those years ago, and he had surprised himself by asking her name during their first dance. 'June', she had replied warmly, 'what's yours'.

Like the Palais and the Maison in Stockton, the Linthorpe Assembly Rooms had long since ceased to be used for dances. In the early sixties, the big dance floors, flashing lights and amplified pop records of the night club and the discotheque, offered more than the revolving silver ball of the dance hall. They provided a more exciting form of entertainment for the teenager, and the Assembly Rooms had been reborn first as a Bingo Parlour and more latterly as a Fitness Centre. Horizontal bars covered it's walls now, and mirrors reflected rows of straining sweat covered club members, all intent on keeping fit by punishing themselves on the exercise machines and weights equipment which covered the original polished wooden strip flooring. A whole new generation in a whole new world. A new plain suspended ceiling hid the original highly ornate plaster mouldings but the small alcove where the resident band played on a raised dais was still there. They had come together shortly after serving with the RAF during the war and called themselves 'The Quadronnaires'. Base, trumpet, piano and drums, hence the name. Good musicians each and every one. He could still picture them in their immaculate Air Force blue blazers and the melodic tunes of the time came back to haunt him, 'In the mood', 'Blue moon', 'These foolish things', 'Autumn leaves'....... Also still in place was the balcony supported by that large column in the middle of the floor, which by tradition, couples had gyrated round in an anti-clockwise direction in a swirl of skirts and outstretched arms and elbows.
Something was missing though. Something that would complete the mental picture. Then he had it. Yes, the rotating glass globe with it's myriad of tiny silver facets. The very epitome and centrepiece of every dance hall, and the focus of every movie about them, it had spilled an ever moving circular pattern of coloured lighting on to the walls and ceiling, and the entwined couples on the darkened floor below. 'We didn't know what to do with it when we moved in, so we just left it hidden behind the new lowered ceiling when we converted the place', the manager informed him, 'it seemed a shame to skip it'.

He recalled the scents and smells of those more innocent times and that familiar musty odour came to mind. A mixture of stale air, perfume and cigarette smoke. It had been a time when smoking was both the macho thing for men and the fashionable thing for women. After all everyone in the movies seemed to do it and they set the fashion. The clutch of crisp white 'Senior Service' or 'Craven A' cigarettes fresh from the packet, all neatly arranged under the gold band of the monogrammed silver plated cigarette case, together with the matching cigarette lighter so carefully filled with lighter fluid, were an essential part of the evenings equipment. They would all be gone at the end of the night of course, lit up in ritualistic fashion at the appropriate time. As a voluntary non smoker now he involuntarily cleared his throat at the thought of all that inhaled tobacco smoke.

Looking down over that once familiar balcony he recalled the occasional church social dance that he had attended in his self conscious early teens. The boys had sat uneasily on one side of the church hall and the girls expectantly on the other, but few had the nerve to cross over the space between until it was time to go home. Later when he realised that the dance hall was one of the few places where boy could meet girl, he had taken a couple of lessons at one of the many schools of ballroom dancing that were popular at the time in the Linthorpe area. The lessons helped, but that what we have to learn to do we learn by doing and his first hesitant request for a dance with a complete stranger came to mind. Someone who was more sympathetic looking than glamorous he had told himself. Someone a little older perhaps. Someone who might be more tolerant of his restricted but well rehearsed steps and limited nervous conversation. In short his lack of experience in such matters. 'You can hold me tighter you know luv. I won't break'. It was all so embarrassing. It was the first time he had sensed the feel of a woman's undergarments, either over or under their outer clothing. The problems and the unease did not really diminish with experience. The embarrassment of the averted eyes of someone who took your own across a crowded room, or sometimes the need to avert your own from the eyes of someone else. Someone you had seen before. Someone you had danced with before. Nice face, pity about the legs....
He had not been assured enough to easily accept rejection in those days. 'Can I have this dance please'. After stubbing out a cigarette and adjusting the tie, the long lonely walk to the other side of the dance hall to make that uncertain enquiry when the next dance was announced was all so polite in those days. Any refusal though could severely dent the ego. An even longer walk back could be even lonelier. How he had envied those who were more dance hall wise and had the courage to make a more positive approach when, 'Are you dancin' might be answered with, 'Are you askin'.
He had acquired but few skills in ballroom dancing at the time - or any time

since then for that matter. To him and all his pals it had always been a means to an end rather than an end in itself. Early in his adventure he had learned that Victor Sylvester's basic 'quick quick, slow slow' routine could be readily adapted to the popular quickstep, foxtrot or waltz, but once on the floor for an announced dance, there was no guarantee that it would not be followed by the dreaded tango or some other Latin American beat when there would be many apologies for trampling on your partner's feet. 'Do you want to sit this one out then'. In an effort to improve his skills he had secretly practised a few basic steps in front of the mirror at home, but he quickly came to appreciate that dancing would never be one of his better accomplishments.

Faint hearts never won fair ladies, but original chat up lines and general conversation, like the dance steps themselves, could be a real problem. Particularly when trying to concentrate on both at the same time. 'Do you come here often', was an old chestnut but nevertheless a popular line for openers, and 'Sorry', figured quite regularly in spoken communication after colliding with some other equally inexpert couple or treading on your partner's toes. 'Would you like a coffee', would be a logical part of the repertoire after a couple of dances but few would venture the hoary and more risque 'If I said you had a beautiful body would you hold it next to mine'. It was difficult to be original. The longer the silence the more the self-conscious, and the more the self conscious the more difficult it became to be original.
It was all made a lot easier of course with an alcoholic beverage or two before the dance. He recalled the many faces and names from those times but in this connection that of Charlie came particularly to mind. A man of influence was Charlie and someone to be forever associated with 'The Rooms' as it was affectionately referred to. No alcoholic drink was served at the dance. He was the man on the door who issued 'pass-outs' to those who wished to imbibe at the local pub, and many wished to imbibe. For them, for better or worse, closing time became dancing time. 'Remember lads, no re-admission after ten thirty'. Tall and lean and always attired in dinner jacket and bow tie, he lent an air of respectability to the occasion. Forever patrolling the entrance foyer, he was always on hand to sort out those who might be causing a minor disturbance after their visit to the pub. His acquaintance was essential in obtaining late tickets for the popular Christmas and New Years eve dances when pass-outs would be in even greater demand - and a return before ten thirty could never be guaranteed.

In an age when both men and women began to wear the figure hugging blue jeans which are still so popular today, he recalled the regulation dark suit with white shirt and tie and the alternative navy blue jacket and grey flannel trousers, which most young men wore before the arrival of the teddy boy culture, when these would be replaced by jackets with velvet collars, ruffled shirts, drainpipe trousers, fluorescent socks and crepe soled shoes. In this new world of growing promise and prosperity, the girls wore layers of frilly petticoats under pleated gingham skirts with extremely flat shoes, or the more sophisticated off the shoulder dresses with absurd high heels. Pointed breasts under tight fitting jumpers were popular at the time, and painted nails and bright red lipstick complimented back combed heavily lacquered beehive hairstyles. When they danced the more energetic jive or jitterbug the more observant voyeur might be rewarded with the glimpse of a stocking top. Sadly enough such visual delights were soon to vanish with the introduction of the more practical though less revealing tights, but this sad change in female attire was not confined to this country. Over here as in America a new breed of music loving teenagers began to appear. They were followers of 'Ole blue eyes' himself, Frank Sinatra, and were referred to as bobbysoxers, after the knee length stockings they were given to wear.

So many memories of so long ago. The short damp Winter afternoon was drawing to a close when he left the premises and it had started to rain. A light drizzle that settled annoyingly on his forehead and glasses as he hurried to his car. Driving back to his office, cocooned in the comfort of the vehicle, his thoughts turned to the ritual at the end of the night when the music slowed for the last waltz.
Oh, the agony and the ecstasy of it all. The effort at sobering up in the last chance saloon. 'Can I take you home'. The girl's likely rebuff or the occasional surprising assent. The noisy scuffle in the men's cloak room to find the duffle coat with the gloves and scarf stuffed in the pockets before meeting up with her again in the noisy lobby. So many people. So many coats, ten and more to a peg, so many more on the dusty floor. The invariable long walk to her home in all weathers and the indecision as to whether it would be better to hold her hand, put an arm around her waist, or simply chat as though you had known this stranger for years. The arrival at the gate might be rewarded with a brief kiss, or there might be a more lingering one on the doorstep, and if you were lucky, there were both. Any speculative straying of the hand inside the coat to areas above the waist might be accepted, but any attempts at investigating those unfamiliar regions below would be gently but firmly resisted. There might even be the promise of a date the following week. A meeting at Rea's ice cream parlour or the pictures perhaps. The Elite, Gaumont or maybe the Odeon, to see 'High Noon' starring Gary Cooper, or 'Doctor In The House' with Dirk Bogarde, hopefully with the possibility of further exploration in the dark intimacy of

the seats in the back row. Then the even longer lonely walk back in the early hours of the morning long after the last bus had gone, the mind filled with thoughts of what had been done, what had not been done, and what might be done on a future occasion.
He smiled at his recollections. How times had changed since those more innocent days. There were rules and values and an unwritten code of conduct then, but all that would change with the arrival of the swinging sixties when life would never be the same again.

'You'll never guess where I've been today June', he declared when he arrived home later that evening with that rotating glass globe still on his mind, 'and guess what, I know where we can get hold of a light fitting that will really give a bit of a sparkle to our Lounge extension.........'

*"A gypsy woman came into the shop one day and said that I would marry the manager". My mother and father before they were married - circa 1924.*

*My father and I in the back garden of the terraced house in Tavistock Road shortly after I was born - 1931.*

*Mam and I shortly after our return from the Midlands - 1944.*

*We did our own rejoicing in the street on VE Day - May 1945.*

*I discovered that I had a talent for drawing buildings but I wasn't sure if I could design them. Bootham Bar Gate, York.*

*I sketched the glory that was Rome during a study trip in 1961.*

*"I discovered that I had a talent for cutting hair and was early elected as tent barber. Christmas Island 1958 - at the time of the British Nuclear testing programme.*

*All dressed up and nowhere to go........*
*Christmas Island, 1958*

*My second hand Ford Consul, It became my pride and joy and went everywhere with me.*

*Our Ford Classic. The car with the big boot - ideal for all the family, 'Are we there yet, Dad....'*

*My young son and daughter soon discovered that dad could draw and I produced a whole range of caricature characters for their amusement. 'Bertie Barrel the Bouncer from Barnes' and below - 'Two-gun Slim Jackson from El-paso'*

# 6. A TALENT FOR DRAWING BUILDINGS

*If few can claim to be happy with their lifetime's work, how many of us I wonder can claim to have been happy throughout the work in their lifetime. I was no star pupil, but with less than average results in my School certificate examination I was fortunate to have been blessed with a certain talent for drawing. What I lacked in the sciences was compensated for by what I might achieve in the arts. In the event I was fortunate enough to pursue both through the practice of Architecture. A pursuit that has opened many doors to people and places....*

❖

Contrary to popular belief schooldays were not the happiest days of my life. I have to say that I didn't learn as much as I should have done at school. Perhaps as a schoolboy I wasn't taught as well as I should have been. I believe children peak academically at different times for different reasons, and I think I was the rule to that belief rather than the exception. I achieved only passable marks the first time I sat for the school certificate, and only marginally better ones the second time. 'He will have to spend less time on football and more time on studying', the Headmaster had told my father after the first sitting. With the benefit of hindsight and mindful of the money footballers earn today, it might have been better to have spent less time on studying and more time on football. Eighteen of us then in three rows of six in a small timber hut especially set up for the purpose. I can still put names to the faces of many of the boys in that final class of forty eight all seeking to improve on their first effort. Having met up again with a few of them since those pre GCSE times, I have discovered strangely enough, that many of those who were expected to achieve great things have found only mediocrity, and some of those who were considered only mediocre have achieved great things.

Sport dominated out of school hours. If football was the dominant game, then tennis provided the opportunity to mix with the opposite sex and experiment on the fringes of it. We played on the courts in Albert park on long warm Summer evenings and flirted in Rea's ice cream parlour afterwards - and sometimes elsewhere. One particular evening one of the girls invited me back to her house to play a strange game called 'pennies'. Sitting on the couch in the front room a little later, I discovered that it involved taking turns to hide a penny in various articles of each others clothing. The object of the game was for the other to find it. The penny was never put anywhere particularly private and nothing untoward occurred, but it was exciting at the time. I felt somewhat special to be selected for such an event, but to my dismay, I discovered later that I was not the only one who had been singled out to find the lucky coin, and I was never invited to do so again. Perhaps I wasn't as daring in my choice of hiding place as I should have been....

Fortunately for me, the marginally better marks in my second sitting of the examination included one for art, which opened the door to Art College and the possibility of a future in commercial art. Free at last from the harsh confining routine of school, at a time when George Orwell's new novel 'Nineteen Eighty Four' portrayed a chilling prophecy about a restricting life in the future, I found a new found freedom in a mixed group of like minded students who were interested in living only for the present. I was introduced to such strange and diverse activities as costume design, pottery classes, lino cutting and sculpture, and visited a large number of museums to draw animals and the like and where, revelling in my passage to manhood, I indulged in good deal of innocent flirtation. With the absolute need to draw the human body accurately, I learned about it's bones, muscles and joints, and saw my first nude figures in life drawing class. It all seemed quite natural and impersonal when the models disrobed for the first time and the classes soon became routine.
The models in question were a younger middle aged man and an older middle aged woman, and I came to the conclusion quite early in life, that after a certain age, the human body whether male or female is not a pretty sight. We unfortunately lack the all covering dense fur coats of the feline family, which serves to disguise the effects of gravity and hide any imperfections. Without the fine silk like coat of such mammals, the attractiveness of the human form relies heavily on subtle means to support it, and even more subtle cover to promote it. The full monty was definitely not for me then - and neither is it now.

Later that first Summer eight of us spent a week at Butlins, Filey. A milestone event without parents. When Sir Billy Butlin opened his first holiday camp at Skegness with it's endless rows of wooden chalets as early as 1936, he surely could surely not have imagined just how popular his idea of providing accommodation, meals and amusement, at an all inclusive price was going to be. In an era before the jet engine revolutionised air travel and made it possible for anyone to travel to the other side of the world, and at a time when expensive packaged holidays to the Meditteranean sun often involved a long uncomfortable flight in a noisy world war two Dakota, the holiday camp provided an ideal affordable holiday for young and old alike. Eight of us then. Four boys and four girls. Inevitably, we paired off shortly after our arrival, but the girl I had fantasized about fancied someone else, and I was left to take up with someone who had fantasized about me. Unfortunately the feelings weren't mutual so I learned little more about the opposite sex that week. The time, like the circumstances, were opportune, but the inclination was absent. The opportunity to find out just what went on under those layers of frilly petticoats and at the top of those seemless nylon stockings, passed without incident. Such things would have to remain a mystery for this red blooded male a while longer.

Our parents need not have worried about their own absence though. In an era before the destruction of the social fabric and the family life that supported it, there was a time for everything and everything was in it's time. Life was so much more innocent then. This was a time before the media covertly encouraged promiscuity and society blindly accepted it. A time before young people uncovered the parts you shouldn't see and covered the parts you should, and when there was a moral code which encouraged young ladies to keep their legs together. A time before condoms were commonplace, the morning after pill became the norm, abortion could be obtained on request, and nearly a half of our children were born out of wedlock. Little did anyone realise at the time, just how far the next generation would push back the boundaries of what was and what was not acceptable, and just how tragic the effects of pushing back those boundaries would be.

In the event our week passed happily enough. 'Good morning campers. Wakey, wakey. Hi-de-Hi'. The Viennese Restaurant, Regency Ballroom and Gaiety Theatre are long gone now, as are the lovely legs, knobbly knees and glamorous grandmother competitions. Gone also is the plastic make believe world of the Hawaii Beachcomber bars where drinks were served by grass skirted girls, and the lounge bars where you could happily watch bathers make faces at you through the walls of the glass sided swimming pools whilst sipping a half shandy. They have all been replaced by attractions much more in keeping with today's higher expectations. Like the days of lost youth however, I'm sure they hold fond memories for many of my own generation, as do the Redcoats and the wealth of information transmitted regularly over the public address system.

'Goodnight campers. See you in the morning. 'Ho-De-Ho'.

A short while after came my first doubts about my future in commercial art and my first thoughts about a career in Architecture. I discovered that I had a talent for drawing buildings, but I wasn't sure that I had an equal talent for

designing them. What we learn to do we learn by doing. Ever concerned about my career, my Father made some enquiries as to how I might launch my new interest, and I was eventually taken on as a member of unpaid staff with a local firm of architects. My change of heart, to some extent, had been inspired by the buildings that were proposed for the Festival of Britain, the impressive Royal Festival Hall, the spacious Dome Of Discovery and the towering Skylon, but any thoughts I may have cherished about working in a modern office and involved with such prestigious buildings quickly evaporated.
This was a time when austerity prevailed, the Offices Shops And Railway Premises Act was still a glint in the unions eye, and a decade before the challenge to pre-war values. The establishment and the class system still ruled OK. It was still possible to recognise what level of the social strata a person came from by the way they spoke, and someone with an upper class accent was someone to be treated with deference. There were still rules of behaviour and that deference was still the fashion. I referred to the partners as 'Sir' and like the rest of the staff, routinely treated them with a great deal of respect. To stand with a hand in your pocket at any time was judged to be discourteous, and to stand with two hands in them was considered slovenly. I should know because they were whipped out of mine by one or other of the Partners on a number of occasions. Thankfully there is little left of that old order now but many of the idols in our new order are not without blemish. In today's society where much of what was once considered important has been reduced to triviality, and much of what was once trivial is now considered important, many of our icons are those who can be the most rude, sometimes crude and on occasion, the most disgusting. Flexible hours and informal dress were still light years away. For those who were inclined, the drain pipe trousers, velvet collared coats and crepe soled shoes, which were popular at the time, would need to be worn after work or in the dance hall. In that age before formica and tubular chairs, we sat in more formal collar and tie working on wooden drawing boards with wooden tee squares. I shared a cramped converted rear room which overlooked a back street, with two other occupants and an indifferent single radiant gas fire, where it was invariably too hot, too cold or too stuffy, and where on occasion the atmosphere was too volatile. Fortunately, if it was not too windy, we were able to open the windows in the summer months. At such times, above the clatter of their machines, we could hear the girls who worked in the clothing factory opposite, singing along to 'Music while you work' which was broadcast every morning on the BBC's Light Programme.

My work was largely concerned with mundane alterations and extensions to existing buildings, which required to be measured up before plans

showing proposals could be drawn up. up. Over the next couple of years, I progressed from holding the end of the tape to reading it, and to eventually being entrusted to prepare the final drawings of the proposed work. If this wassomewhat repetitious however, the building surveys often provided an insight into some of the prevailing post war slum conditions, in which many in a certain social stratum of our society were obliged to live at the time.
As a somewhat green and sheltered teenager, schooled in the belief that mendings, cleanliness and good speech are respectable, and rags, dirt and bad language are offensive, I was easily shocked when I first saw household coal in a bath. Unfortunately the state of some of the premises we had cause to visit, showed less consideration for sanitation and hygiene and more for ease and convenience. In such conditions we were often obliged to light up cigarettes to disguise the strange and unpleasant odours that permeated such places. On one memorable survey, we discovered that the owner of a small corner shop in Cannon Street who used a horse and cart for delivery purposes, kept the animal in the back room. That entire street and all it's original shops have long since gone. Gone also has the hard working but law abiding way of life of the poor but proud people who used to live over them. They were moved into the new council estates to start a new society and a better way of life, but strangely enough, many would claim that they left behind values which had prevented society from falling apart . It is ironic that forty years on, despite the best efforts of the government, town planners and the city fathers, many of those once neat and tidy law abiding communities have become unruly council ghettos, where the inhabitants live in fear by day and are afraid to go out at night, and which even the police patrol at their peril. So much for on going post war government's policies of welfare dependency, state support and more latterly, unswerving political correctness. Policies which suppress motivation, remove the work ethic, encourage fraud and promote dependency in young and old alike. The only real satisfaction in life is achievement, and the sad fact is that whole generations are not been given the chance to achieve anything in a compensation culture which is costing us all. So much for progress.
Life did however have it's both lighter and enlightening moments. I recall one occasion when I was warned not to venture alone into a local shirt factory. 'You'd better come with me', the foreman advised, 'some of the girls working in there will have the trousers off you for a laugh if the mood takes them, and oh, don't mind their language'. So much for the gentle fairer sex. So much for their gentility.

To accompany this broadening of the mind came a six day working week. Despite a combination of office work on weekdays, evening classes at night, and study at the weekend, there were events to relieve the monotony and

stop Jack becoming a dull boy. These generally involved some serious Saturday afternoon football, and some equally serious Saturday night drinking before the Saturday night dance. With the jet engine ousting the propeller, a great deal was happening in a shrinking world that was altering out of all recognition, but like others of my age group, I was more interested in Roger Bannister and The Busby Babes than the Suez Crisis and the Hungarian Revolution, though the billowing skirts of Marilyn Monroe in 'The Seven Year Itch', and the nakedness of Brigitte Bardot in 'And God Created Woman', stirred more than the imagination at the time.
I recall the historical day of the Coronation when the weather typically gave little respect to the historic event. It rained most of the day, and I spent a good deal of it watching the proceedings on the television in the home of a trainee nurse I had met at the previous Saturday night dance. It had been a hasty arrangement at her front door after a long walk to her house. I needn't have bothered though. She seemed more interested in the events in the Abbey than she did in me that day, so I left early and returned home to find my family and friends gathered round the television set, only interested in much the same thing. I suspect that for many of them it may have been the first time they had watched television. Like the public at large they had been captivated by an historic event which for the first time had been brought directly into their homes. John Logie Baird's television had finally come of age. Life would never be the same again.

With the dawning of the new Elizabethan age came the realisation that I needed to gain more work experience, and with more work experience came the realisation that it was time to move on. When the opportunity came to take up a post with J.G.L. Poulson who had recently opened a branch office in Middlesbrough, I took it. I believed his was a large practice which handled some impressive projects which I could learn from. Unfortunately my career move proved to be a poor one. The impressive projects remained at his head office and I learned little about them. For myself, I can neither confirm nor deny the accusations which were subsequently levelled against the man, but suffice to say, on the rare occasions that we met, I found him to be less of a professional and more of an amateur, less of an architect and more of an opportunist. A hire and fire man, he hired me to work in his branch office in Middlesbrough, and fired me six months later when I refused to leave home to work permanently at his main office in Pontefract on the same salary.

In the event the timing was opportune. The more things you leave to chance, the less chance there is for you. I had already applied and been accepted for a post in the Engineering department at ICI in Billingham. If I

had not been sacked I would have given in my notice anyway and this time the move proved to be a good one. I moved on to a four figure salary, the magical one thousand pounds per annum. Wow.... My new found status prompted me to take my driving test and my father to invest in a family car. I could now join the new elite who drove to work. But time, like imperial measurement, was running out. While Bill Haley and his Comets were rocking round the clock, I began working round it in an attempt to complete my intermediate studies before National service claimed me.
Having achieved this goal, I wasn't too surprised when a buff coloured envelope marked On Her Majesty's Service dropped through the letter box one Winter's morning, requesting me to attend a medical examination. I had heard that the ability to march a long way in large boots was essential to service life, and a part of me had hoped that I might have flat feet or other such debarring afflictions, but I could only boast a flat stomach and I was duly pronounced A1 and fit for service. For the first time in my life I felt that I had no control over my immediate future. The time yet to come was as unknown to me as the space which the Russians had blasted a satellite into that same year. In a strange twist of fate many of my friends and colleagues, who hoped to see a bit of the world, had been accepted for the RAF Regiment. Ironically enough they had received a home posting, and spent a frustrating two years in defence of the realm striking each of their 370 days of service off a demob calendar, and hitching lifts on the A1 to get back home on thirty six hour weekend passes. I on the other hand was refused acceptance to the RAF. Having little wish to travel, I was posted abroad with an Engineer regiment to see a part of the world I would rather not have seen. Little did I realise that in company with hundreds of other unsuspecting peacetime conscripts, I was destined to be posted to the wrong place at the wrong time, to fight an unseen enemy on the other side of the world - and write a book about my experiences afterwards.

There has been, and probably will continue to be, much talk about the value of National Service and the merits of introducing it into today's society, to bring a bit of much needed discipline into the lives of the many undisciplined and lawless young who blight our inner cities and invade our homes. In spite of - or maybe because of - the brass, the bull, and the bullying, National Service did teach a lesson in comradeship, moral principles, acceptable standards and human behaviour. It separated the men from the boys, turned the boys into men, and made them more accountable.
I do not believe however that many of the young men of today could cope with the harsh disciplinary regime of two years National service, neither do I believe that Government could enforce such vote losing conscription now. There have been too many profound changes in Britain since those more

patriotic times. Much of the Englishness has disappeared from our every day lives, and with it, much of the loyalty. There was an order, dignity, and honesty to life then, a structure and morality to everyday life. We have fed too long at the table of self indulgence, gorged too much on instant gratification, and digested too many European directives to accept such an intrusion into our lives now. Having had so much we expect so much more. I'm sure that if we opened Pandora's Box now we would expect to find glad tidings of great joy. I doubt moreover whether the ethnic population would respond to such legislation now. The recent support - or lack of it - which the tens of thousands of additional new immigrants who enter the country each year give to the English cricket team, is indicative of where their allegiance really lies. The quintessential significance of Edward Elgar's stirring music, William Wordsworth's romantic poetry, Charles Dicken's creative novels or Harry Wingfield's paintings in the popular Ladybird books, is understandably lost on them. I suspect that even the great majority of the indigenous population would surely claim that to sacrifice two years of their young lives was an infringement of their human rights. I'm sure that any envelope dropping through their letter box would be ignored, and I'm equally sure that the Government could do little about it.

June and I made the decision to become engaged shortly before I left for training. I had met her the year before at a Christmas eve dance at the Linthorpe Assembly Rooms. A meeting place where many a local groom met his future bride. At such festive times it had long been customary for my pals and their girlfriends to go back to my home to party afterwards, and during the last dance I had hesitatingly asked her if she wished to come along. One memorable attraction of these early morning festivities, was the delicious pork and stuffing buns which my mother always prepared and thoughtfully laid out for us before discreetly retiring for the night. Such was their popularity that they took only second place to the necking sessions in an unlit room which invariably followed the party games. When June agreed to go out with me again later in the week I wondered whether it was me she fancied or more of my mother's pork and stuffing buns.

The greater part of my National service in foreign fields is well chronicled elsewhere. With hula hoop mania making the world go round, I was making the most of what I could on the other side of it. If there were few emotional farewells on cold station platforms there many letters of endearment afterwards. In our case absence did indeed make the heart grow fonder and the despair of my leaving was matched only by the joy of my homecoming. I rather liked the idea of a shared wardrobe and stockings in the basin when a fellow needs a shave and we were married shortly after my return to civilian life.

# 7. THE BRASS, THE BULL AND THE BULLYING

*Between 1945 and 1963 nearly 2.3 million young able bodied men between the ages of eighteen and twenty four were called up to complete two years of involuntary National Service in the armed forces. There were no exceptions. They came from all walks of life. Those who were enlisted from the slums rubbed shoulders with those from public schools. Deprived of family, wives and girlfriends, they were all were subject to a draconian like discipline and taught to blindly obey orders in the gruelling regime of basic training. Some were victimised and some went sick with nerves, but most benefited from the experience and survived with broadened minds to learn the true value of discipline and respect for others and themselves.*

There were noticeably more young men on the train the closer it got to Farnborough. Young men from all walks of life, each with their own subdued look, each with their own thoughts, and each with the same questioning look on their fresh young faces. None carried a great deal of personal luggage, but like those in my carriage, each clutched a small suitcase which they would need to return their civilian clothes in once they arrived at their destination. Involuntary National Service had claimed them for two years as it had finally done for me, and with that suitcase would go the last vestiges of their civilian lives.

Hesitant as strangers are in such circumstances, the conversation amongst those occupying my carriage was hesitant and strange.

'You going to the same place as I am mate', said one. 'Have they called you up as well. I don't know why they put me in the Engineers. I put down for the Catering corps. The girl friend thought I would have a better chance of coming home for the weekend. Do you want a sandwich'.

'Strange that', said another. 'My older brother's a mechanic. He put down for the Engineers and they put him in the Pioneer corps. I thought about joining the Merchant Navy. Where you from then'.

'A pal of mine did his National Service with the Royal Engineers', yet another announced. 'He said they did special training after square bashing learning how to build bridges and clear land mines. He told me you can't beat the system and to keep my head down and not volunteer for anything. I've heard the food's awful. Are you married'.

I told them how I had put down for a different service. Like many of my pals, my National service had been deferred for some time so that I could continue

with my studies. They had gone in to the RAF Regiment to do their National Service. They seemed to have survived relatively unscathed and it seemed natural for me to follow in their footsteps, but that particular avenue had closed when discovered that I would have to join up for three years. Having declined the Queen's shilling to become a regular in the RAF to defend their airfields, the Ministry of Defence decided in its wisdom that I could best serve the realm by becoming a Sapper in the Royal Engineers to do something else.
True to form we received our first taste of the stern Army discipline that was to follow from a glowering Sergeant when, in the falling rain and the fast fading light of a short January day, we alighted nervously from the train at Farnborough station as raw recruits.
'All right then, let's have you. You're in the Army now. Get fell in over here at the double you lot. Shortest on the left, tallest on the right', he barked before we were bundled unceremoniously into the back of a three ton truck that was waiting to take us to the camp. 'Come on, move yourselves'.
It was a cry we would hear a lot over the next fourteen weeks. Goodbye freedom, welcome to confinement. Like Elvis Presley's UK hit of the year, we were about to be all shook up in an unholy cocktail of brass, bull and bullying.

During our short stay at Farnborough we were kitted out and sorted out in a short induction course that was to prove a prelude to the shape of things to come. It was here that our identity was reduced to an army number, we were issued with our kit, and informed that all losses would have to be paid for. We soon learned that small, medium and large was the Army's only concession to bespoke tailoring and nothing fitted perfectly. There were many of course whose measurements fell somewhere between these parameters, and their coarse brown uniforms tended to fit where they touched. We discovered that army underclothes were both uncomfortable and very impractical and best worn back to front, that drill practice and marching in boots quickly made holes in the heels of woollen socks and wounds all heels, and the only way to bring an acceptable smooth gleaming shine to the toe caps of your best boots was with the aid of a hot iron and a great deal of spit and polish. We were introduced to such diverse equipment as a housewife and button cleaners, and soon learned that a good deal of our miserly Army pay went on Brasso and Blanco. In a typical catch 22 situation these essential items could only be obtained at the camp NAAFI, which also proved to be the only place where anything edible could be found, and where egg and chips and beans on toast soon proved to be a rare delicacy.
'The sardines on toast are off luv, and that's the last jam doughnut'.
Immunised and traumatised we learned that cleanliness and

orderliness were paramount. At a time when Brigitte Bardot was baring all for the first time in the mainstream cinema, many were baring all for the first time in the communal showers. In an effort to put us off sex for the duration, we were treated to a gory film showing the horrendous effect of having unprotected sex with an infected person, and the painful treatment that was required should you require it afterwards. It was rumoured that bromide was being added to our tea to dispel any lingering ardour, but we had no way of knowing if this was true. It is strange how a rumour without a leg to stand on has no difficulty in getting around.

In the spirit of inspiring loyalty and instilling a common sense of purpose, we were given lectures on the history of the Royal Engineers, informed of their many battle honours, and the role they played in the nation's wars, but freshly plucked from hearth, home, and in some cases mother's apron strings, such facts did little to persuade raw recruits to be too proud of the famous Badge on their berets so early in their new careers.

We were woken in our billet at the same unearthly hour by a Sergeant in the same crude fashion. At six-o-clock on a freezing Winters morning I would sometimes have to pinch myself to prove that I wasn't still dreaming or on the film set of 'The Way ahead'. It was a completely new shock to the system

'Come on you 'orrible lot. Rise and shine. You might break your mother's heart but you won't break mine. Out of your pits, hands off cocks and feet into socks'.

Each frosty day, as a foretaste of things to come, we showered and shaved in an unheated ablution block to satisfy hygiene standards, and ate terrible food in the cookhouse to satisfy a constant hunger. Any complaints about the food were met with a mild disbelief. Bemused by names, ranks, flashes and uniforms, we failed to salute those we should have saluted and saluted those we should not have saluted. We were made to look inferior on parade and even more inferior in the gymnasium. When we were not involved with some activity or other we were changing our clothing in preparation for it or cleaning and ironing it afterwards. We heard the sound of men breaking wind and the 'Eff' word more times than we had heard it in our previous lifetime, and soon learned that we were expected to obey orders instantly and never answer back, and that a minor mishap of one could lead to severe punishment for all.

Each bitterly cold night after each strenuous day, we heaped as much coke as we could on the single stove which glowed red hot in the centre of our billet, before collapsing exhausted onto our beds. Understandably, for some reluctant young recruits, the ordeal of these early days proved to be too demanding. In the darkness after lights out I could sometimes make out the red glow of that last comforting Capstan full strength cigarette of the day, and on occasion, I could swear I heard the faintest sound of sobbing from the more homesick.

After two weeks of such indoctrination we were taken across country by train to another training camp, but if we thought that our transfer from Farnborough to Malvern wells was the beginning of the end of our training, it proved to be only the end of the beginning. The training camp at Malvern Wells was the place where the story really began. It was here that we finally lost touch with the outside world for six weeks. It was here that the men were separated from the boys and attempts were made to make us or break us. It was here that we learned to hate the more tyrannical of our instructors who made enemies of us all with their continual verbal abuse and demeaning orders, and it was here that we learned that the army had a way of doing everything and everything had to be done economically.
'Remember you only use three sheets of paper to wipe your arse lad. One up, one down, and one for the splashes'.
There were twenty of us or so to a billet, each of us close shaved every day and shorn of hair twice a week. We were inspected every morning by the Corporal in charge of the hut who always declared that we needed a shave and a haircut. Each man had a bed and locker and at any time the cry of 'Stand by your beds' usually meant stand by to be humiliated. No one was exempt. Forever ironing and creasing, pressing and cleaning, buffing and polishing, there were times when we believed we were being trained for housekeeping rather than soldiering, but predictably enough, our best cleansing efforts could never satisfy our instructors.
'Your bed space is filthy. There's dust everywhere. When did you last clean this bloody mess tin Sapper. I can see the remains of your breakfast in it. Don't you like the food here, or are you planning to eat it later. Are these your best boots. Is this supposed to be your best BD. They're disgusting. Are you trying to make a fool out of me Sapper'.
'No corporal'.
You're a filthy idle man aren't you. Stand to attention when I'm speaking to you', and then eyeball to eyeball, 'What are you'.
'I'm a filthy idle man Corporal'.
Sometimes the entire contents of a locker, together with the kit so painstakingly arranged on the bed, would be tipped on the floor before our tormentor moved on to his next victim who would be made to endure the same humiliation. Sometimes the fire bucket would be kicked over in a final show of aggression as he left the room.
'When was the water in that fire bucket last changed'. There's life forms in it'.

Each day followed each repetitive day in what seemed like a never ending round of parades and inspections, and each day we were crudely informed by all and sundry that we were the worst bunch that our instructors had ever had to deal with. There was no time to stand and stare. We marched everywhere, usually at the double.
'Come on move yourselves. Smallest on the left, tallest on the right. By the left - quick march. Left, right, left right.... Come along, come along. Pick it up at the back there. Who's that man out of step. Take his name Corporal.'
A minor offence could often result in a ridiculous punishment which usually involved carrying heavy loads in full kit over great distances, either early in the morning or late at night - or both. Orders of the day were posted on the camp notice board and this had to be checked every day. Not looking was no excuse for not knowing, not knowing was a chargeable offence, and a chargeable offence could result in a spell in the 'glasshouse' where the white capped military police were less than courteous. The most onerous discovery was that of selection for overnight guard duty. Everyone got a turn, the more unfortunate more than once. No one was exempt and the inspection before we marched off to the guard room was daunting. The general comments on our turnout by the Sergeant Major were laced with expletives and directed at us, whilst those of the officer of the day were invariably directed at the Sergeant Major. The inference being that he should do something about it, and he invariably did the following day. Two hours on and two hours off, it was a long uncomfortable night. Fully dressed in uniform on an uncomfortable bunk bed, any sleep was fitful, and there was always the possibility of a familiar call at some unearthly hour if the officer of the day felt inclined to pay us a visit.
'Fall out the guard. Come on. Move yourselves....'
We did a one off eight mile route march which put blisters on the feet, and had a day working in the cookhouse putting blisters on the hands. We spent a good deal of time inside in the gymnasium, where I never mastered the art of climbing a rope or vaulting a horse, and outside on the parade ground, where I could never carried out the drill movements to the satisfaction of the Drill Sergeant Major. He was a man who struck terror in all our hearts. He was a law unto himself and I was not alone in living in perpetual fear of dropping my rifle or bayonet - or both - on parade. He had a voice like thunder and a face to match when the mood took him, and the mood took him often.
'Slope - arms, shoulder - arms, pre - sent - arms, fix - wait for it, wait for it - bayonets'. Every command was done by numbers, and in the spirit of co-ordination we were loudly encouraged to loudly shout the numbers out.
'One, two, three - one, two, three - one, two, three....'
We drilled in ranks of three. Many struggled to take up a position in the

middle rank in the mistaken belief that any mistakes wouldn't be noticed, but he had eyes like a hawk, and we soon realised that those who had done so received his special attention.
'Get into three ranks. Come on you idle lot, move yourselves. Right - dress. Number off . Squad, atten -tion. Right - turn. By the left, quick - march. Left, right, left, right....
Setting an unauthorised foot on his hallowed parade ground was strictly taboo. When his cries unexpectedly bellowed across it everyone within earshot froze to the spot.
'Who's that 'orrible little man with his hands in his pockets. I'll have you lad'.

Weapons training brought a few surprises when we nervously fired them in the rifle butts for the first time. I discovered that the trusty 303 Lee Enfield rifle kicked back quite sharply when it was fired and needed to be tucked well into the shoulder to avoid any bruising, that it's barrel had to be regularly boiled out with water and pulled through with an oily rag, and the Bren gun besides being very noisy, was also liable to jam. I also learned that a close grouping of shots was better than a spread of them, and after my rifle had been zeroed in by the armourer, I found that I could group them close to the centre of the target. The fact that I could shoot at all was a surprise to me. I had never had much luck at the fairground. That worthless prize on the bottom shelf had always eluded me, but this time there was to be a worthwhile prize of a different sort. It was usual at this time of year for the intake to send a team to compete at Bisley, the small village in Surrey noted for it's annual meeting of the National Rifle Association, and much to my surprise I was selected to be a part of the team. I can recall the drizzle on the day which disconcertingly blurred the vision through my army issue spectacles on occasion, but not the event for which I proudly - and unexpectedly - collected a silver spoon.

For six weeks distracted day followed distracted day. There was precious little time left to seek out the limited comforts of the NAAFI, or anything else for that matter. Letters from wives and girlfriends were eagerly awaited and read over and over again, sometimes in private, and sometimes unashamedly more publicly. At a time when Pat Boone was all the rage and writing his 'love letters in the sand', we were scribbling ours by return in great haste with his postscript 'I'll be home'. Most things are unbearable until you have them to bear, but intimidated and shouted at all day by bullying instructors as we were, many felt disorientated and even victimized. In such circumstances a 'Dear John' letter didn't help our situation. Under such draconian discipline, where any minor indiscretion could result in even more shouting and intimidation, perhaps it is not surprising that some found themselves unable to comprehend orders and sought the counsel of the vicar after church parade. Others went sick, some suffered with nerves, and a few went absent without leave only to be hunted down and later brought back to camp like a criminal.

The great majority however went absent with leave on a thirty six hour pass after eight weeks of basic training. Dressed again in civilian clothes the respite was short and it was sweet, but the luxury of a comfortable bed, good food, loving arms and tender talk, was all too soon replaced with a further six weeks of field engineering under the same stern regime we had endured before we went on leave. We learned how to tie granny knots, reef knots and other knots, and in the process very often tied ourselves in knots. We were instructed on how to build Bailey bridges over swollen rivers, clear mines from soggy fields, and place booby traps in toilets and other unlikely places. It was hard work over long hours, in all weathers, sometimes at night, and having never been called on to lift anything heavier than a pencil during my Architectural training, my entire body disagreed in every way with what the army's idea of what constituted a 'one man load'.
Whilst the Russians were putting their sputnik into space, we were putting the finishing touches to our kit, in readiness for the final inspection which took place before the passing out parade at the end of our training. Nothing less than immaculate was expected. Since there would be little time in the morning for such perfection, we decided to thoroughly clean the billet and our bed space and lay out our kit on our beds the night before, and sleep on the floor in our greatcoats beside it.
We held a party to mark our pass-out and the completion of our training. It turned out to be quite a wild affair. During the celebrations, one of the more abusive Lance Corporal instructors was unceremoniously hurled into the very lake we had done our bridging exercises over by a person or persons unknown. Notwithstanding his demeaning orders I felt a little sorry for him when I heard the news. I knew he had fought in and lived through the terrible Korean conflict. He may have had a cruel streak, but he knew his weapons. When the noisy Bren gun jammed in the heat of battle, he would be the one person I would want beside me to unjam it.

We went on a weeks leave the following day. When we returned we were put into a Holding and Drafting unit where we saluted everything that moved, painted everything that didn't, shovelled a great deal of coke, and peeled a large number of potatoes until our postings had been determined. We also pondered on our future. We knew that most of us would be posted to Germany and I had resigned myself to that scenario, but horror of horrors, I discovered that for some reason I had been selected for even more punishing training. I was to be subjected to a further eight weeks of intensive 'square bashing' to qualify as another unpopular training instructor. Why me I thought, I hadn't been particularly good at anything and I considered my drill as being particularly bad. Postings are normally written in stone. To this day I don't know how I managed it, but somehow I eventually convinced the Commanding officer that I would be better employed in another capacity, and I was eventually posted as a draughtsman to 38 Corps Engineer Regiment which was stationed in Roberts Barracks in Osnabruck, Germany. When I arrived there however it soon became apparent that there would be precious little draughtsmanship. Throughout that Summer I took part in a lot more parades and bridging jaunts and a taxing week long NATO exercise, a war game when I lost a lot of sleep and a good measure of morale. I might have taken part in a lot more, had it not been for a chance meeting with a Sergeant in the Education Corps who suggested that I put in a request for a transfer. 'It's teaching the three R's really. There's few inspections and you don't need to wear boots. You'll have your own room and a lot more free time'. I needed no second bidding. I'd had enough of Bailey bridging and I decided that I would cross any other bridges when I got to them.

Having passed the course and duly qualified as an education instructor, I returned to the camp in Osnabruck happy in the expectation that things would be different. Walking up to the guard room on that early evening in November 1957 however, I could never have visualised just how different things would be. Little did I realise that fate was about to direct me elsewhere, or how traumatic that elsewhere would prove to be.
Where've you been, Sapper?' barked the Corporal of the Guard, catching sight of the insignia on my battledress. He was obviously surprised to see me.
'I've been on a training course near Hanover for the last five weeks, Corp'.
'Have you now. Well, 38 Regiment's gone back to Ripon. Seems they've gone without you. They're off to Christmas Island soon. You can bed down here in the guard room tonight and see the Adjutant in the morning'.
The news left me completely dumbfounded. Why on earth was the Regiment going to Christmas Island, and where was that island anyway. Just when you think you can make ends meet, somebody moves the ends.......

# 8. NOTHING PREPARED ME FOR WHAT I SAW

*I had no experience of long sea voyages at the time of my National Service. A short ferry trip across an indifferent channel from time to time represented the full extent of my seafaring experiences. When I joined an Engineer Regiment based in Germany, little did I realise that, along with hundreds of other servicemen, I was destined to take a long sea voyage to a little known Island in the Pacific ocean on the other side of the world. The Island was to be used in connection with the British nuclear testing programme, and fate had decreed that the Engineer regiment and I were to be a part of it. Little had prepared me for the voyage, but nothing had prepared myself or anyone else on the troopship for the terrible storm that we encountered in the Bay of Biscay just two days after our departure from Southampton....*

Her majesty's troopship 'Dunera' was an elderly, single funnel, converted cruise ship of some 37,000 tons, her once sparkling white paint now streaked with rust. She towered above the wharf, and as I made my way up the gangplank I could make out the clutter of transport and other military equipment lining her upper decks. This would be the vessel that would sail nearly ten thousand miles in four weeks, taking myself and the Engineer Regiment to which I had been posted, across two oceans to a lonely place on the other side of the world. To a place that would be forever associated with a British nuclear testing programme and later bring it's own controversy. Standards of accommodation on the vessel had been provided strictly in accordance with the pecking order of officers, NCO's and other ranks. I soon discovered that along with other humble Sappers, I had been allocated sleeping quarters on a deck whose portholes were just six inches above the water line, and on an upper berth bunk bed where the ceiling was just six inches above my head. It was hot, cramped and claustrophobic. When we left Southampton around midnight on the 30th December on a cold, still, clear night, and slipped silently into the Solent, the wake of the vessel lay like a ribbon of white lace on a calm sea in the soft moonlight.
'I hope it's as smooth as this all the way there', a young soldier remarked shortly after our departure, 'I get seasick on a rowboat'.

We received little warning of the terrible storm we encountered in the Bay of Biscay on New Year's day. We had spent a strange and nostalgic New

Year's Eve having a few beers and playing card games in the saloon which had been allocated to other ranks. Despite the significance of the date on the calendar most were in a subdued mood. We talked nostalgically about what we were doing the previous New Year's eve and exchanged photographs of the wives and girlfriends that we had left behind. Under the circumstances there seemed little cause for celebration and most had retired thoughtfully to their berths shortly after midnight, oblivious to the turbulence that would shortly mark the beginning of a turbulent year.

When we woke the next morning there was a distinct pitch and roll to the ship which had not been apparent the night before. From the position in my bunk I could see that the portholes were more often than not below the water line. It soon became difficult to stand without some form of support and any thoughts of breakfast disappeared with the first feelings of nausea. During the morning the little routine that had been established was abandoned as the severity of the storm increased. By midday everyone had been confined below the windswept decks and most had retired to their bunks in some distress. Though we did not know it at the time the storm was to greatly increase in severity over the next couple of days and the ship would be pounded by a North Atlantic in it's angriest mood for over a quarter of a century.
On that first day I witnessed the awful effects of seasickness first hand. There were long trails of vomit to the ablutions which many had tried to reach in vain. Few if any bothered about reaching the sickbay, and little could be done about their problem if they had. Some, like myself, staggered around between bouts of sickness in a futile attempt to find some clean outside air, and others just lay fully dressed where they were, in the contents of their own stomach too ill to get out of their bunks. On the sea-swept decks outside, lifelines had been rigged to enable the luckless crew members to go about their duties, and one can only imagine the agony of those who may have been as much prone to seasickness as we were. There had been one lifeboat drill and our lifeboat station identified before the storm, but I dread to think of the confusion that would have ensued had we needed to reach it, or the difficulties there would have been in actually launching a lifeboat in those extreme conditions - if they could have been launched at all.

The storm continued for the next three days and soon developed into a force of nine to ten on the Beaufort scale, when each North Atlantic roller sent a disturbing shudder through the ship as they pounded her broadside on. I recalled the ship's apparent size and it's cliff like sides from the time we boarded her, but here she was being pitched and rolled on every wave like a cork. In such circumstances we rightly call upon God, but we row away

from the rocks. I learned afterwards that such was the concern of the captain about the roll of the ship on the second day of the great storm, that he gave orders to cut loose much of the heavy equipment and vehicles on the upper deck for more stability in the heavy seas.
Below decks there was little or no discipline. General disarray and disorder were everywhere. There was no one to give orders and none could have obeyed them if any had been given. There was no sight of an officer or an NCO, for the angry sea made no exceptions and they were reduced to the same wretched physical state as everyone else. Nothing was cleaned up and no one cared whether it was. Such was the agony of some that it was obvious they could not have cared less if the ship were to sink, and I suspect there were many more who would have voiced the same belief if they could have summoned up the energy to do so.

There was little difference between night and day and to all it was totally irrelevant. To those like myself, restricted below decks, where the smell of sickness pervaded the fetid air, only the soulless bulkhead lighting revealed the true pitiful physical state of ourselves. No one was exempt, and there were times when I wondered how that young soldier who claimed he was sick on a rowboat was coping. The portholes in our sleeping quarters had been bolted shut by the crew at the first signs of the changing conditions, and other than a continuing swirl of grey-green water little could be seen through them now.
Above the cries and groans of those who were now beyond being physically sick, came the creaks and groans of the ship, and occasionally the crash of something else breaking loose from it's lashings. Anything and everything that could break did break, and anything and everything that was not secured, rolled to and fro on the fouled floor. Above us was our saloon. One night at the height of the storm, a large piano which had been secured broke free from it's lashings and, with each roll of the ship, careered from one wall to the other smashing into the timber wall panelling eventually destroying the entire contents of the room.
No one thought of food. The idea of eating anything was abhorrent and no one ventured to find out whether any food was being served in a canteen which was empty for days. Someone said that we should be drinking a lot to avoid dehydration, but few had the will or the strength to do so.

On the morning of the third day of the storm, in a desperate effort to get a little fresh air and away from the mayhem below, I followed a member of the crew up a companion ladder which gave access to a lower outer deck. With some trepidation I opened the deck hatch door a little and looked out, but nothing prepared me for what I saw. There was no horizon as stormy sea

and leaden sky merged together in a dull grey mist and spray. The sea swept decks, now empty and deserted, appeared as if in another world, and little could be heard above the howl of the gale force wind which threatened to pull the very door from my hand. To one side I could just make out the vague outline of the bridge and superstructure and a blur of navigation lights on the heaving mast head. For a fleeting moment I wondered who could possibly be in control of such a wayward vessel and how was it possible to make headway in such conditions. Perhaps at that time we were not making any headway at all. Away to the port side I could see that yet another wall of grey-green water with a foaming, curling crest and which I judged to be about forty to fifty feet high, was bearing hard down on our vessel. Not daring to look further I pulled the hatch door firmly to and waited. A short while later the giant wave announced it's arrival with a familiar sickening thud as it struck the vessel broadside on, and as it did so an acre of steel plate and a multitude of rivets took the strain. The ship shuddered with the impact, rode the crest of the wave for a moment, shaking off thousands of gallons of water, before sliding down the other side in preparation for the next onslaught. What the eye doesn't see the mind doesn't grieve about. Having seen enough and having no wish to see more, I closed the hatch door and quickly retreated to the confined but more familiar surroundings below deck mentally thanking the builders for producing such a sturdy vessel.
'What's it like up there?', someone ventured to remark when I returned.
'You don't want to know' , was all I could muster by way of reply.
Silence is often the gratitude of true reflection.

On the fourth day when all had given up on the storm ever ending, it suddenly abated. When it did there was great deal of cleaning up to do. A week or so later we had left the treacherous cold grey waters of the North Atlantic and were sailing across the calm warm blue waters of the Caribbean. In complete contrast to a violent ocean and restless storm clouds, we looked through our now open portholes across a mirror-like sea reflecting a clear blue sky. It felt good to be alive and well, and allowed on deck to enjoy the fresh air. The canteen became a popular venue again. Young men recover quickly - and so do their appetites.

# 9. A LOOK INTO DANTE'S INFERNO

*On August 6th, 1945, the first atomic bomb was detonated over the Japanese city of Hiroshima. It's terrible effect brought an end to the second world war. With the cold war which followed came the arms race and the policy of producing ever more destructive weapons as a deterrent to future wars. By the late fifties, ever more intent on self destruction, the ingenuity of man had produced a weapon a thousand times more powerful - the hydrogen bomb. A weapon which threatened the very existence of mankind. Christmas Island had been selected to test this terrifying new means of mass destruction before the global ban on nuclear testing came into effect, and fate had decreed that I, along with hundreds of others, should be a witness. The operation was codenamed 'Grapple Y'. Tragically enough, in later life, many of those young witnesses would have to grapple with the haunting consequences of their imposed duties on that island. They would become the victims of the irradiation sting in the grapple bird's tail. The Ministry Of defence has a lot to answer for....*

'Forty seconds'. The countdown came from a tannoy system which had been crudely rigged on a nearby mast. In company with hundreds of other fellow servicemen, I was kneeling on some open scrub covered sand, facing away from the direction of the forthcoming explosion of a hydrogen bomb. As if to come to terms with the magnitude of the moment and my own sense of vulnerability, my thoughts were drawn back to my boyhood years when it seemed that I finally grasped the enormity of the approaching explosion. In my mind's eye I recalled the Allies' development of the 'tall boy' or 'earthquake bomb' as it was called, which caused so much terror and destruction in the closing stages of the second world war. I recalled the cinema newsreels at the time and the sight of the adapted Lancaster bombers of Bomber Command weighed down as they were with these massive destructive payloads, clawing their way into the darkening skies on route to reaping bomber Harris' promised whirlwind.
That conventional bomb was the equivalent of ten tons of TNT. The nuclear weapon which at that very moment was falling from the dawn sky had an explosive power of three million tons of TNT....

It had all started earlier. A lot earlier. Around two-o-clock that morning in fact. In those dark unfriendly humid hours, we had made our way to the cookhouse where we had an early breakfast, and collected our 'survival rations'. These could be life saving, we were informed, should the RAF 'Valiant bomber, which had been adapted to drop the weapon. crash on take off. Should this happen radio active material would be released, and it would be necessary to evacuate the Island on ships that had been moored a safe distance away.
A couple of hours later, complete with our minimal survival kit, we boarded the three ton trucks which took us to the first assembly point upwind from the airfield, where we remained until the aircraft was safely airborne. With the plane safely in the air and well clear of the Island we were again ordered into the three tonners and taken to our final destination. A safe place upwind again from the dropping point, which was ominously referred to as 'ground zero'.

A beautiful, still dawn had broken a little earlier, heralding another now familiar hot, sunny and humid day. Looking round I could see that several hundred of us were grouped on an open, low scrub-covered area of sandy ground. Between us and the dropping point was our transport which was parked on a narrow dirt road under the trees of a coconut plantation. Beyond the plantation was a lagoon. The tannoy system kept us informed of progress but the waiting created a nervous atmosphere. There was nothing to do and most were silent at that early hour. Some tried to make light of the situation with amusing comments and a few ate their survival rations for something to do. We were all aware that the aircraft, with it's deadly cargo, was somewhere above us in that clear blue sky, but it could neither be seen nor heard, and the only sound was the occasional crackle of atmospherics from the tannoy. At around 7am it suddenly sprang to life and the unseen announcer calmly informed us that the weapon had now left the plane. With but thirty seconds to detonation we were told to kneel down, face away from ground zero, and to close and cover our eyes.
'Thirty, twenty, ten', the countdown continued from the tannoy. Out in the open as we were, with no protection, hearts were beating faster now. In those final moments I was overtaken with an awful feeling of vulnerability, and a natural inclination to run away and seek some form of shelter. We had been told what to expect during earlier rehearsals, but this was the real thing. Like all the wildlife on the Island, oblivious to the events that were about to unfold, there was no where to run to now.
'Nine, eight, seven, six, five', and thoughts of that awesome weapon falling at a thousand feet per second filled my mind. How close was I to ground zero I wondered. What if it fell closer than planned or exploded at the wrong

height?. In those final remaining seconds I could sense these and another hundred questions on the minds of the silent, apprehensive hunched bodies grouped silently around me.
'Four, three, two, one, zero'. For those whose eyes were not so tightly closed and not so firmly covered, was that tiny glow real or imaginary. Perhaps there was a flicker of light, otherwise nothing. An ongoing count upward commenced.
'One, two, three, four, five....'. For some time we knelt in complete silence and anti climax. At around plus fifteen the voice on the tannoy informed us that we could if we wished look towards ground zero. Curiosity got the better of me. When I shaded my eyes and turned nervously round I was presented with a terrifying look into Dante's inferno. A giant flaming orange ball of fire and boiling gas, connected to the ground with spiralling shoots of red and brown debris, was swirling and turning in upon itself, climbing ever higher into the clear blue sky. At this early morning hour an awesome second setting sun had suddenly appeared on a horizon, now devoid of the small white clouds that had been evaporated in the fierce heat of the explosion. It had a fearful and alien fascination which filled the mind, the sky and, it seemed, the entire universe. Still no sound. The silence was deafening. An eerie calm prevailed for what seemed like an age as most stood in awe of this frightening show of man's ultimate destructive force. The count up continued. At plus twenty the tannoy warned us to stand by for the heat and blast wave, and the noise of the explosion.
It began with a low grumbling sound from afar, continued as ten thousand horses of the apocalypse, and finished as an ear splitting crack of doom, a foretaste of Armageddon, in what seemed like an eternity later. A terrifying rack of thunder as if to signal another day of judgement and the end of the world. The ground shook and the ominous noise rumbled on around as the blast wave hit us. Those who had unwittingly stood up desperately struggled to keep their feet, and some were felled by the violence of this man made storm as it spread ever outwards from it's epicentre. The air was full of raging hot dust, sand and flying debris, and in the maelstrom the palm trees in the plantation some distance away bent through almost ninety degrees and showered the trucks parked underneath with their coconuts.
With the blast came the heat wave, perhaps the most frightening effect of all. For a few seconds there came an intense concentration of heat on uncovered parts of the body, the momentary radiation of heat from an open furnace door, a fearful concentration of energy to match the fireball. For an instant, looking down, I could imagine a fusion of the coral sand in the sensation of the moment. Out of the corner of my eye, I saw someone cross himself as the now rapidly forming sinister mushroom shaped cloud appeared about to envelop us.

Many back home had seen pictures of the previous nuclear tests on the television screen back home, but none could have possibly imagined the ferocity of such a release of energy. Never before had Albert Einstein's celebrated equation $E=MC^2$ been more frighteningly demonstrated. We were truly witnessing the dark side of human invention.
'God that was close', muttered a white faced young soldier next to me, nervously reaching for a cigarette. Under the circumstances it seemed reasonable to call on the almighty.
'You have to see, hear and feel it to believe it', someone else pointedly remarked.
Through it all the tannoy had continued it's upward count. At plus forty the deadly gaseous cloud had begun to take up it's familiar shape as the top spilled over itself to climb thousands of feet into the air. The dark mushroom like silhouette, stark against the sky, would hang there for some considerable time before it's tenuous links with the ground would be broken and the top begin to break away in the prevailing wind, carrying with it we hoped, any radiation away from the Island and out over the Pacific.

We stood in amazement for a long time on that stretch of sandy scrub, gazing at the sky, before it was considered safe enough for us to board the trucks that would take us back to Main Camp. Relieved of normal duties, we were left to cast the occasional worried look at that evil omen of cloud which persisted in the sky for rest of the day, and reflect on the earlier traumatic events which had made such an indelible impression on all who had witnessed them. Many had been left speechless, but I was inclined to agree with the comment made by a colleague who I found kneeling next to me just after the passing of the heat and blast wave, when he observed with some emotion, 'If there were to be a nuclear war then I think I would want myself and my family to go early'.

The following morning we woke to a familiar blue sky with no trace of the ominous mushroom cloud. For most, as onlookers, the events of the previous day were an awesome experience which would be remembered for a lifetime. For others directly connected to the test, the more hazardous work was just beginning. For some, whose more direct duties were carried out with little or no protection, warnings or safeguards, the tragic consequences would manifest themselves twenty and more years into the future, and haunt them for the rest of their lives.

# 10. ARE WE THERE YET DAD

*Many would claim that it all really started in 1886 when Carl Benz was granted a patent to develop a three wheeled 'motor carriage' which proved to be an outstanding success. Walt Disney once said 'If you can dream it, you can do it', and in 1908 Henry Ford took the first step to realising his own dream of making a four wheeled vehicle that everyone could afford when he first dreamed up, and later produced, the first 'Model T'. The 'Tin Lizzie', as it was affectionately called, was the world's first motor car to be produced on an assembly line. Mass-produced and mass-marketed, it would be 'a motor car for the great multitude', he claimed and 'they can have it in any colour they want as long as it's black'. Apparently that was the only paint available at the time that dried fast enough. It's production was an immediate success and so began the Western world's twentieth century love affair with the motor car.*

❖

Travelling on public transport only teaches us to shove our neighbours. For the first time in our history, the motor car allowed us to travel in comfort where we want, when we want, how we want, and with whom we want. We could travel with ease as we pleased. We have come a long way from 1905, when the AA was formed to combat the growing hostility to motorists who were frightening men and horses alike. Cities and towns were quieter then and more rural like, but revolutions never go backwards. Despite it's pollution, and tendency to make puddings of us all, the motor car has become a status symbol, a place of seclusion, a private world, and on occasion a place of retreat. It is, at the same time, versatile and compact. It can accommodate children, the elderly and the infirm, pets and luggage, all from door to door in comparative comfort. An unheard of luxury for the vast majority of my previous generation, the motor car has brought a new sense of freedom. For almost a century now, despite the ever increasing cost of motoring, the motor car has continued to be both a source of pride for some and a lifelong passion for others. Both a blessing and a curse, what was once regarded as a luxury for the few, has become a necessity for the many who feel uncomfortable and ill equipped without their wheels.

To each his own. I am no mechanic. Born in the year that Malcolm Campbell seized the world land speed record in his custom built car 'Bluebird', I must confess to going through life knowing little about such technicalities as drag coefficients, maximum torque, compression ratios, tortion beam axles, multi point fuel injection systems and the like. It is all something of a foreign language to me. The finer workings of the modern internal combustion engine is something which I know very little about, and have little wish to know. In earlier years necessity has on occasion compelled me to effect some often crude repair work, but what went on under the bonnet then, remains as much if not more of a mystery to me now, as it does I suspect for much of the general motoring public. At a time when we replace a headlight bulb with a whole new headlight assembly, and make good a small scratch by spraying an entire door panel, it is not necessary to have such knowledge now. This was not so for those of my previous generation, many of whom liked a challenge and sought such perfection as they could from their dream machines. I recall my father-in-law spending days in black oily overalls decoking the family car in a cold garage. It was apparently the thing to do after driving a certain number of miles. Strange thing is I believe he actually enjoyed doing it. For myself, I am a great believer in leaving what works alone. 'Don't ask me I only drive it', is my stock answer to any questions of a technical nature, and I strongly suspect that Concorde captains and Nuclear Submarine commanders say much the same thing.

My own parents never did own a car of their own, but nostalgia does not always bring back fond memories of better times in the good old days. Motor cars were far too expensive for a generation that was not particularly car minded. Theirs of necessity was a world of indifferent public transport. Of steam trains and trolley buses and unheated double decker buses. Before the luxury of a car, I recall travelling to my first place of work on cold, wet Monday mornings on their crowded and smoke filled upper decks. Condensation would stream down the rusting windows in small rivulets, and drip down from the cigarette stained metal roof on to the heads and shoulders of the coughing occupants below. To add to the discomfort, the experience would often be repeated on the return journey home after work, when the odour of damp clothing would be even stronger following a day of heavy rain.

'Can I mind your car Mister'.
Come rain or shine, I must have asked that question many times during my boyhood years. It was addressed to drivers, who, having nowhere else to leave their cars, routinely parked them in the road outside our house on

Saturday afternoons. It was as routine as asking for a cigarette card or a penny for the guy. Living as I did only a short distance away from Middlesbrough's football ground at Ayresome Park, the surrounding streets would be filled with parked vehicles on match days. At such times what the local residents regarded an annoyance, the local youth considered to be an opportunity. The minding effort usually involved no more than a reappearance shortly before the owner returned, when a penny would be a generous reward for so little effort. If the team had won and spirits were high there might be a little more. Not surprisingly, there was no great demand for property around a ground whose sanitation, like most other similar venues of the time, were less than basic. Despite this, or in our case, because of it, my parents had no difficulty in selling our house when the time came for us to move. It was bought by the club for a new centre half they had signed.... The club has moved to a brand new stadium at the Riverside now. It's certainly more hygienic, but they still have parking problems.

After riding through early manhood on two wheels of my bicycle, I went through a stage of limbo before I passed my driving test in the early fifties, to drive on four. A time when the post war car market was just getting into it's stride, and only fifteen per cent of all households had access to a car. A time when radios, when they worked, were just good fun, and heaters were the last word in sophistication. A time when the more popular new innovative smaller range of cars had started to come off the assembly lines. The Ford Anglia, Morris Minor, Volkswagen Beetle and the Citroen 2CV, all had the new flashing indicator lights.
Since it was around November time, I recall that I had taken all my driving lessons after work, after tea, and after dark, when it was invariably raining, and in a car that did not have flashing indicator lights. Strangely enough the driving test proved to be the first time I drove a vehicle on dry roads in broad daylight, but if the improved conditions were a bonus, then the highlight was the unplanned emergency stop. Toward the end of the test, a ball suddenly bounced out of a side street. After bringing the car to an abrupt halt, a young boy, oblivious to any danger, ran out immediately in front of it.
'That will do fine', an ashen faced examiner said, 'I'd like you to take the next turning on the right and return directly to the test centre if you would please'.

Like the cars themselves, the driving test was far less complicated then than it is now. Neither was it so expensive. In another example of the lawful subsidising the lawless, I fear we shall see more unlicensed drivers on our roads as the costs rise and the number of test failures increase.
There is a first time for everything and little matches the thrill of driving

alone in a car for the first time. It is a completely new experience. No one to impress. No one to instruct. No one to criticise and no one to offer advice.

Cocooned in your vehicle and sole master of your situation, you see the world outside from a totally new perspective, and anticipate a whole new respect from it. 'Hey, look at me. I can drive now'. A misplaced confidence however can sometimes result in terrible blunders and often in simple mistakes. People who live in glass houses shouldn't throw stones. If we dig deep enough into our own motoring past, we can all surely remember some silly error made in haste or poor judgement.

Shortly after passing my test, and in the best traditions of the growing band of so called Sunday motorists, I hired a car and took my parents for a day out in the Lake District. The car was big, black, and somewhat bulbous, with lots of chrome trim and leather seating, and a large steering wheel and wooden dashboard as was fashionable at the time. A typical bull nosed family saloon. A car which many British manufacturers at the time believed the public wanted. I recall that I drove many miles that memorable day, up hill and down dale through rain and shine on narrow winding roads without a hint of mishap, only to foolishly scrape the side of the car on one of the brick gate pillars when we returned home after dark.

'It's only a small scratch Jim. Don't worry about it. I don't suppose they'll even notice it'.

Despite the obvious my mother was always reassuring, but worry I did. As I suspected, in the all revealing cold light of the following day, the mishap looked less of a small scratch and more of a large scrape. It was all most embarrassing. It was a long time before I drove a hire car again and needless to say, when I did, it was from a different firm.

My introduction to motoring was at a time when motorists, like society, were more considerate of others, and when there was a smile for every mile. A time when courtesy was extended to the highway, when road rage was unheard of, when it was safe to leave your car unattended, and hitch hikers went unmolested. A time before the overtakers kept the undertakers busy. A time before double yellow lines, cluttered roads, tearaway joy riders, bus lanes, rumble strips and speed cameras. A time when a forecourt attendant filled your petrol tank at the local garage. But as Bob Dylan noted, 'The times they were a changin'. Despite the huge advances in motoring technology, or maybe because of it, that same politeness, discipline and formality, would soon be lost in the brave new world of one for all and all for me.

Fortunately, I still have a few prized dinky toys to remind me of those more nostalgic days. The small Vauxhall Cresta, Austin Atlantic, Morris Oxford and Ford Zephyr replicas are the pride of the collection. Sadly enough, the numerous vintage cars I made from the less durable Airfix Construction Kits and Meccano sets have, like the sets themselves, long since disappeared

My first car was a second hand Ford Consul, the first in a range of the new slab sided models which had just come on to the market. Like the bicycles of my earlier days, it soon became my pride and joy, and always careful to avoid the offending gate pillar, went everywhere with me. We are all slaves to fashion, and whitewall tyres, like two tone cars, were very fashionable at the time. I recall spending a great deal of time and effort meticulously painting the sides of mine with a white rubberised product. Unfortunately it didn't do exactly what it said on the tin, and I spent a great deal more time cleaning it off. Whitewalls or not, it still holds fond memories. It was the car which I did most of my courting in, and I have to say that the innovative front bench seating and steering wheel gear change, made it most admirable for the purpose. Necessity is not necessarily the mother of invention, otherwise the Egyptians would have invented the combine harvester, but from four wheels to no wheels it was also the car we reluctantly had to sell to buy our first house.

My wife June's enthusiasm for cars gives lie to the theory they are a man's thing. I have always considered myself fortunate that we shared an interest in them, and she has kept a record of all the cars we have had. There are notes on their colour, registration number and date acquired in a separate album, and their orderly arrangement is as much a testament to her enthusiasm as her tidy mind. The acquisition of each and every one was always the subject of much deliberation before visiting the forecourt, and often a learning curve on it. Too big, too small, wrong colour, wrong shape, too many miles, too many owners. On rare occasions though the heart has ruled the head and we have been somewhat less than practical. The car that looks so perfect on a sunny Saturday afternoon when viewed at leisure, loses a little of it's appeal on a dark wet Monday morning when it's time to go to work. It's a well known human frailty. Buyer's remorse the car dealers call it. 'Trust me I'm a car salesman'

There have been many cars since the Consul. None have the same wistful memories of course, but every model has it's own place in the family history. Each was a mirror of motoring progress, and each a reflection of it's own time. If the conventional box like Ford Cortina was a popular model which most of my generation seemed to have driven at some point in their lives, then the economical and remarkably spacious Mini was a sensation. A truly British classic, it proved to be the last car to be designed by one person. Ford

produced their own Classic whose boot they claimed was big enough to accommodate an opened deck chair complete with a seated occupant. We tried it, and it did. The Ford Capri, with it's so called power bulge in the long bonnet which has remained a mystery to me to this day, was our first new car. It looked sporty, but with it's low seats and poor visibility, it wasn't the best of family cars and probably looked it's best when it was driven by Denis Waterman in the TV series of 'Minder'. Our lifetime shopping list also included the first of the Toyota Celicas, produced at a time when Japanese car makers, not quite sure what might appeal to the Western market, included just about everything, and the famed Italian Alfa Romeo, which contrarily boasted a beautiful engine and shoddy bodywork.
If the oil crisis of the mid seventies changed the way we viewed our economy, it also changed our motor cars which became smaller and more economical. We acquired a VW Scirocco, with it's revolutionary hatch back design that fused the rear window with a boot door, boosting a new popular aerodynamic shape. 'The desert wind whose heat you will feel', the brochure enthusiastically declared. Ironically when we drove one to the South of France on holiday one year, the mistral blew from the North and it was extremely cold.
Manufacturers have since discovered that the ideal aerodynamic shape for a motor car would match the profile of a half egg. Such a bland profile would have little attraction for the motorist, and the addition of a wheel at each corner would make it even less of an appealing product. Jeremy Clarkson would be appalled.

Like yesterdays British motor industry, all are yesterdays cars now, but each and every one has it's own associations. Many are of fond memories of holidays and day trips to the seaside. 'Are we there yet Dad'
If the weather is not kind in the North east, it is understanding of goose pimples. Between June and September we would wander on to the sand-blown beaches of Redcar, Saltburn and Seaton where, on sunny days and if the wind was from a northerly direction, it was possible to have your costumed body roasted on one side and frozen on the other. We would help our young excited offspring build sand castles, and discover just how cold the North Sea could be when the tide came in to wash all our efforts away. A bit like life I suppose. Nothing in this world is really permanent. I remember the leaking thermos flasks, melting ninety-nines, sticky candyfloss and gritty sandwiches, the animated barking of dogs as they darted between the shallow incoming waves, the excited shrieks of children as they tentatively put a toe in the cold water, the candy striped deckchairs, the uncomfortable donkey rides and the colourful Punch and Judy shows. I recall the sudden downpours of rain that drove everyone into the noisy amusemnet arcades,

the sand which stubbornly stuck between the toes of wet feet, the modesty problems of changing into a dry bathing costume, and the bigger problems of changing out of a wet one. I recollect the saucy Bamforth seaside postcards that could be found on squeaking rotating stands on windy piers and under the colourful awnings of shops on the promenade where you could buy anything from candy floss to lettered 'all the way through' rock and crisp golden brown waffles.
Sometimes we would travel overnight to a more distant resort for an affordable family holiday. It was a time before seatbelts and car seats were compulsory, crumple zones a rarity, air bags only a concept, and air conditioning an incredible luxury. There were no motorways then. With son and daughter fast asleep on cushions in the back seats, and June nodding her head from time to time in an unsuccessful attempt to keep awake in the front, I would snake my lonely way South on deserted A and B roads through the darkened slumbering countryside, alone in my own private world. A rare time of quiet reflection, my thoughts disturbed only by the sound of an occasional passing vehicle, or sometimes by the unusual sight of a rabbit in the middle of the road, momentarily hypnotised in the car's headlights before scuttling off into the adjoining hedgerow. The best things in life are free. When it came the Summer dawn was both mysterious and impressive. As the blue of the night slowly surrendered to the first light of the day, unfamiliar ghostly images slowly took on a more recognisable shape as little pools of mist in the adjoining fields cleared to reveal the familiar countryside once again. With that first light would often come the first stirrings of the sleepy eyed occupants at the rear.
'Are we there yet Dad'.
Magical as they were, I cannot recall seeing many other such summer dawns since. Sadly enough, how many of us urban dwellers can wonder. Cometh the motorway, cometh the madness. Happiness should be a half way station between too little and too much. By good luck and good fortune I believe we have lived through the best of motoring times.

From a motoring standpoint our lives are less complicated now, and have been since our son and daughter flew the nest. There was an earlier more confusing time when each member of the family had their own means of transportation. First we extended the garage, then we extended the drive until there was nowhere left to extend to. Despite these creations, each day brought it's own parking problems. Much like other families really. Two cars to move out and two back again before you left home for work - and the same manoeuvring when you returned home from work. 'I can't move my car out Mam. Can you move yours'. I recall the many problems with rust, usually concerned with exhaust pipes and over wheel arches and around door sills.

The ominous looking unsightly bubbles were usually discovered with dismay when washing the car at the weekend. Like all families we have had some disasters with spray cans, suffered the occasional furtive siphoning of petrol, charged many a flat battery in the garage overnight and made the occasional makeshift repair. One of my son's pals at the time believed he could repair most things with a five pound hammer, and never hesitated to put his convictions to the test.
There were also the usual concerns about our offspring coming home late. Not the concerns of today's lawless gun toting and violent society, when it is necessary for those living in inner cities to ensure doors are locked and windows are secure at traffic lights, but concerns never-the-less. When we discovered that they had a covert arrangement to let each other in we double locked the front and back doors one night. When my daughter returned in the early hours of the morning, my son discovered he couldn't open either of them for her and she had to sleep in her car in the garage. She was never late again.

On matters of mobility we have come a long way in a short time. A little more than a century ago, the distance that those living in rural communities could hope to travel was limited to the distance they could walk during the daylight hours, and many of those living in the urban environment relied entirely on the horse and carriage as a means of transport. Since those times, courtesy of the internal combustion engine, we have enjoyed a hundred years of motoring on an oil derivative fuel seeing and enjoying far away places our ancestors could only dream of. But what of the shape of things to come. In the mid to longer term our planet has finite reserves, but in the shorter term politics may well determine the future. Much depends on whether the oil rich countries, like Saudi Arabia, are inclined to release or withhold their reserves of oil in the interests of the Western economy in general - and our motoring habits in particular.
In 1985 a British scientist warned us that in using up a half of the world's oil supplies, we have created a huge hole in the ozone layer over Antarctica. Unless we can come up with an alternative fuel, we will eventually consume the rest of it and presumably create a hole twice as big. Electric cars and cars powered by liquid petroleum gas have been tried and tested, but they have their limitations. At the present time, liquid hydrogen appears to be the preferred alternative fuel for environmental friendly hydrogen fuel cell cars, but the scarcity of such powered vehicles on our roads is matched only by the absence of environmental friendly liquid hydrogen filling stations. Predictions for the future notwithstanding, Britain's motorists have paid and continue to pay the highest prices for their cars in Europe. Such is our nature that we will continue to complain when we buy them, and such is the

nature of the motor agencies that they will continue to ignore our complaints when we make them. Aided and abetted by traffic planners who appear determined to bring more disorder and confusion on to our roads, Government seems intent on continuing it's hate campaign against both the law abiding town and country motorist alike, and the exorbitant tax on fuel, together with the ever increasing so called road tax, has taught us the fallacy of what goes up must come down. How long before tolls on motorways and inner city areas are introduced, How long before cities themselves become no go areas I wonder, and how long before driving a car in a public place will constitute a criminal offence....

We are not alone. In 1950 there were less than 50 million cars on the road worldwide. Now there are over 500 million, over 25 million in Britain alone with over eighty per cent of households having a car or ready access to one. Ours is a small Island with an ever growing number of car owners with, ironically enough, more than a million of them failing to register, tax, insure or MOT their vehicles. We have already learned that it is often quicker to walk than ride and better to travel hopefully than to arrive, but such is the fondness for and convenience of our cars that we still refuse to use our public transport services.
Surely we cannot continue to cover our once green and pleasant land with more and more acres of tarmac, and reduce our green belts to green ridges. I like to think that we could perhaps take to the air with some form of Autocopter, the dream of Jules Verne, but I dread to think of the rotor blade to rotor blade traffic chaos in the skyways over our cities. The best of all prophets for the future is the past. Perhaps it will all end one day in the nightmare scenario of a gigantic snarl up of traffic on the M25, with long tail backs from it's sliproads all the way back to the inner city, bringing first the capital and eventually the entire South East to a complete standstill. One catastrophic gridlock too many, it may prove impossible to untangle. Bad news for the motorist, but good news for the hedgehogs which are squashed flat in their tens of thousands every year.

Having acquired a BMW I reckon I have reached the pinnacle of my motoring ambitions now. It's not very patriotic I know, but you have to give the Germans a grudging respect. Other than two world wars they don't get too much wrong and as Herr Kipling might say, they do make an exceedingly good range of motor cars.
In one sense June and I have come full circle. On occasion, in the Summer months, we take our grandchildren on day trips to the seaside and other places of interest, regular haunts of ours in the fifties and the sixties. Journeys of discovery for them and nostalgia for us. The route, the scenery,

the resort and the motor car itself have changed a lot over the years of course, but some things will never change. Nearing our destination, when the novelty of getting there has worn off a little, we can always rely on the customary interrogation from the rear occupants.
'Are we there yet Grandad'.

# 11. MANY HARD DAYS NIGHTS

*Someone once said that you should get your happiness out of your work if you would know what real happiness is. When I qualified as an Architect 'to promote and facilitate the various arts and sciences connected therewith', little did I realise just how difficult and at the same time how rewarding life would be. To remain constant in the same job will put a stop to most careers, but given the circumstances surrounding mine, I found the proverb to be true more by accident than design.*

In a psychedelic decade when the Beatles prompted a whole new style of haircuts, neat suits and distinctive music, and James Bond gained his licence to thrill, I passed my qualifying examination and obtained my own licence to practice Architecture.

I could have gone to university and completed my studies the easy way in three years, but I chose to keep my position at work and qualify the hard way in twice as many. It wasn't easy juggling work, study and family. New to the ups and downs of parenthood, my young son and daughter soon discovered Dad could draw, and I spent as many hours drawing at home for their amusement as I did drawing at work for a living. It was a time when 3-D images and holograms were all the rage, the space race produced the first non stick frying pan, the newly liberated woman wore Mary Quant's micro skirts, hot pants and platform shoes, and stopped preparing home cooked food. At a time when hippies and the flower power fraternity were suggesting that we all make love and not war, I worked most nights and into the early hours of most mornings normally too tired to do so. Whilst Harold Wilson was promising a new Britain forged in the white heat of scientific revolution, I worked on an old drawing board, set up on an improvised dressing table in the front bedroom of the modest bungalow we had bought shortly after we were married. Under such circumstances I saw little of the white heat and even less of the scientific revolution. The climate was more seasonal with long cold winters then. Squeezed to arrive later and depart earlier with each year that passes, they are far milder now. It was normal to toboggan down Bell Hill after a heavy fall of snow, and skate on the frozen lake in Albert park during a hard frost. It was also a time before the new National Building Regulations came into force to restrict the licence of speculative builders, and before a new breed of Building Inspectors appeared to strictly enforce them. Central heating was a luxury we couldn't afford, cavity wall insulation a novelty, and double glazing a future innovation. On many a hard days night I worked in my overcoat wearing mittens. My breath would hang in the air and in the morning it was not unusual to discover that the curtains were frozen to the single pain of window glass. Despite these trials and tribulations my efforts eventually brought there own reward and, like LBJ who went all the way, I became a man of letters when I was elected an Associate of the Royal Institute Of British Architects.

Though it is not possible to qualify outside of university now I have never regretted qualifying through the ranks as it were. An Architect does not work in a vacuum. He does not work in isolation. Indeed the exact opposite applies. He must liase closely with a number of other professionals throughout the design stage, and eventually with the contractor who erects his building. He is responsible to both the client who commissions him and the community at large who, unfortunately, seem to know little of his responsibilities and even less of the extent to which he influences their lives. Many would claim that to learn first hand about such things at an early age in an office environment in tandem with study, is a great advantage. As for creative design itself, I believe it's something you cannot really learn. Form follows function and you've either got it or you haven't.

In an age of pin-ups, pop art, punk rock, purple jeans and the pill, I recall the nail biting climax to the world cup in 1966, and the shared sense of elation that engulfed the nation when England won the competition. My father and I watched the game on television from the edge of our seats that memorable day, eating the new fangled defrosted convenience food and drinking tinned lager. The English were a proud race at that time and justifiably so. The football team that triumphed wore the England shirt for the honour it brought to both them and their country, rather than the financial riches it later brought to their counterparts. As a keen supporter of our national team however, I have to confess to being somewhat confused as to their country of origin now. Since the most recent census form makes no reference to an English nationality, how is it possible to have an English football team. In a land that once proclaimed itself to be the home of the beautiful game, the three lions on their shirts must be just as perplexed as myself. Paradoxically the players in the team that represents us in international competition appear to have an English club but no country. Who exactly are we cheering on I wonder.

My qualification prompted some further thought for the future. When the opportunity came to join another local firm of private Architects in Middlesbrough with the prospect of becoming a junior partner, I needed no second bidding. I joined for the usual reasons of course. Better prospects, promotion, a more varied and interesting workload, and of course - a better salary. Money does make the world go around and after all, we're all a little mercenary at heart if we're honest. Since Architects offices are invariably of the same mould, and the Architects and their Assistants who work in them are by custom of the same inclination, I soon became accepted as one of the team, and sporting long hair, longer sideburns and even longer kipper ties as was fashionable at the time, I worked many hard days nights. I discovered just how breathless I could be when I played my first game of five-a-side football with the office team. Many young men of my generation had sown the seeds of their tobacco habit during their years of National Service, and I was no exception. Since the crispy weed could be readily obtained in tins of fifty at a time at hugely subsidised prices in the NAAFI both here and abroad, perhaps it is not surprising. I cannot remember just how and when I gave up the habit but I certainly played harder and longer when I did.

Working hard and playing hard, there was a real confidence in the office about the future. But things are rarely as they seem. Expectation often fails when most it promises and with the arrival of the miners strike, the ensuing power cuts and the three day week, that confidence in the future proved to be misplaced. Before King Faisal's momentous oil embargo of October 1973 gave lie to the dream of an ever expanding Western economy based on a continuing supply of cheap oil, there had been no shortage of work. While Mohammed Ali rumbled in the jungle and the nation watched Uri Geller mind bending his spoons on television, we had watched the practice grow with a host of new commissions, but in 1976, with energy costs soaring as high as the temperatures in the relentless heat wave which hovered over Europe that year, the economy moved into recession, the practice moved from boom times to bust, and the new commissions evaporated. Such was the situation that, in order to secure the future of the Practice, ambitious plans were laid to seek work in the Middle East. Like others in the office at the time, I had some reservations about having to leave a familiar hearth and a comfortable home, but I believed it was necessary to do so in order that I had a familiar hearth and comfortable home to come home to.

It was about this time that I experienced my own early mid-life crisis, what the more learned Scientists today might refer to as the Maleopause. I'm sure all us males get it in some form or other at some time in life. I didn't suffer from hot flushes, but I did sleep badly and I developed a healthy rash on my arms and legs. I also became severely depressed and felt a great need to retreat into myself. All the symptoms of stress the doctor said at the time, which is odd really, because I had never felt that I had been stressed at any time. Do we ever know about such things until it is too late I wonder. Maybe the Scientists are right when they claim that men do become hormonally challenged in mid life. When they are faced with a combination of mounting financial commitments, overriding problems at work, and other responsibilities. In the event I resolved to take my work less seriously and give my health a chance, but it proved to be a resolution easily made but not so easily kept. What is this life so full of care we have not time to stand and stare.

The difficulties and rewards of working in an alien environment in the heat and sand of the remote Emirate of Ras al-Khaimah on a bachelor basis, and my thoughts on what we could and should learn from Islamic customs and culture, before Stanley Kubrick's Clockwork Orange mentality takes over our urban society, are well chronicled in my second book, 'Tide Of Fortune - Time Of Change'.
History shows that there has always been a conflict between Islam and Christendom and it is unfortunate that, whilst the time honoured Islamic and Christian faiths aspire to the same moral principles, there still remains a great divide between the two cultures as, for the first time in our long history, we seek to integrate them into our multi cultural society. Neither are perfect, each have their limitations, both have their values. If we are to have a peaceful co-existence, one must learn to respect the other. As the struggle in the middle East to find a rightful homeland for the homeless Palestinian people continues, perhaps the best that we can hope for, is that both the Eastern and Western fundamentalists will come to realise the folly of violence and intimidation to achieve their aims. Perhaps the coming together of both faiths in our country will help to bring about an elimination of the worst of the excesses and the practice of the best of the moral values and philosophy that can be found in both.

Despite my status as a Junior Partner I learned that the highest branch is not always the safest roost at times of extreme adversity when, shortly after Prime Minister Jim Callaghan declared his naive innocence of any crisis in a strike bound country, I faced my own crisis when I was made redundant and joined the ranks of the unemployed. Like many others at the time, I soon discovered that the one thing that hurts more than paying income tax is not paying income tax. The initial novelty of laying in bed and not having to go to work on cold and wet Monday mornings was quickly replaced with disturbing visions of an impoverished future for both myself and my family, and the realisation that someone had to pay the mortgage. Like most men I found it difficult to come to terms with the fact that I was no longer the provider. In an attempt to supplement my meagre unemployment benefit, which under the circumstances I had no reservations about claiming, I early accepted the offer to photograph the best of the buildings designed by my former practice only to discover the difficulties of photographing them at their best. I knew a little about lighting and balance, composition and framing, but I invariably discovered that the ideal photograph had to be taken from the middle of the main road, during the early morning or late evening rush hour, when it wasn't raining, and the sun was shining from a cloudless blue sky. Frustration, thy name is photography.

Fortunately enough, with Caroline and Christopher at school all day, June had managed to secure a full time job as a receptionist in the newly opened Captain Cook Museum. Located as it was in a somewhat remote place in Stewart park, it was dedicated to the memory of someone who discovered remote places. The role reversal proved to be as whole a new experience for me as I'm sure it did for others in my situation, and in it's own way for Dennis Thatcher when his wife became Prime Minister earlier that year. Wandering from room to room as the mood took me in those lengthy unaccustomed daylight hours, I felt somewhat of a stranger in my own home in a strangely silent world. Between my contemplative wanderings I continued my quest for suitable employment. Whilst an ice cool Borg was wowing the Wimbledon centre court fans with his ground strokes that summer, I was wowing prospective employers, near, far and wide, with a curriculum vitae which in desperation grew ever more impressive after each failed interview.... It was a worrying time, but being somewhat of an optimist by nature, I have always tried to persuade myself that the glass of life is always half full rather than half empty, that things only work out if you work at them, and opportunity does sometimes come knocking at the door when you least expect it. And so it proved. With our finances reduced to one further mortgage payment, my confidence in the future was somewhat restored when I secured a post with a well known practice who required an architect in their overseas branch office in Doha, the capital city of Qatar, where the inhabitants were being rocketed into the twentieth century on a commercial tide of oil. It meant leaving home again, but with the future still looking a bit of an unknown quantity, it appeared that once again I had little alternative but to journey into a foreign clime.

If my first venture into the Middle East to help establish a practice was somewhat dramatic, then my second visit with an established practice was more rewarding. To some extent I had already learned the hard way in this

land where 'Inshallah' (God willing) everything would be done 'bukra' (tomorrow). I knew a little about what to do and what not to do. Where to go and where not to go. What is considered polite and what is not. I had already experienced the reality of the fierce heat when temperatures could soar to over a hundred and thirty degrees at midday in the Summer months, and the debilitating effects of the high humidity throughout the year. I knew it was impossible to eat, sleep or work without air conditioning. I was aware of the troublesome flies, the biting cockroaches, the rabies ridden dogs and the occasional scorpion. I appreciated the care needed both as a pedestrian and a driver, and the need to stay on the road when driving over the desert, particularly in the dark when a collision with a camel could often prove fatal. I knew a little of Arab etiquette, the difficulty of understanding the Arab language, the problems of pronouncing it and the near impossibility of learning it.
More importantly, I was aware that Islamic law reached into every aspect of Arab life and their severe but simple moral code was based on a clear distinction of what is right and what is wrong. Unlike our society, theirs was a justice of an eye for an eye and a tooth for a tooth. The punishment rightly fitted the crime. I understood that I would be only a guest in their country and there would be no exceptions for misguided Europeans who abused their hospitality.

Though far from home I soon adapted once again to a lifestyle which grew on me, and of course it was paying well. There was a time near the end of my contract when I considered whether I should take a permanent post and bring my family out to join me. Should I become a true expatriate I pondered. Why should I wish to go back to the UK with all it's red tape and needless bureaucracy I began to ask myself. It looked a violent place from where I was and it was always cold and raining. I was well paid for a job that I enjoyed doing and I didn't pay tax. The figure in my monthly statement was what I received. I had a well appointed air conditioned flat in the centre of the city with a houseboy to do the cleaning, and an air conditioned car. The weather was perfect for half of the year and I was rapidly acclimatising to the other half. It all seemed to make an excellent case for not returning to the UK, but I felt that politically things were about to change and subsequent events proved me right.
When I did finally return home to an unknown future there were things I wanted to forget, but there were other things that I would never forget. The tall distinguished looking Arab men with their strong aquiline faces, heavily lidded eyes, narrow jaws and pointed beards, working worry beads in the long slender fingers of their fine hands, and the Arab women in drab black garb, their looks and sensuality shrouded in mystery. I will recall with

wonder the musical sound of the holy men calling the faithful to prayer at a spectacular dawn or a striking sunset, the noise and confusion and insistent babble of the 'souk' (market place) where a sweet musky odour of perfume and oils asserted the senses, the custom built 'dhows' [fishing vessels] bobbing gently at their moorings on the unbelievable aquamarine coloured waters of the gulf, and the singular beauty of the endless wind sculptured desert sands. Such memories will always be with me.

With one half of the world the world waiting to find out who shot JR and the other half trying to discover the original pattern on Rubik's cube, I once again I found myself unemployed. The eighties was a decade of material possessions when money was chasing goods. Fashion and style were available to all. If you had it you flaunted it. Your place in society was measured by the possessions you had, and there was plenty of possessions to be had by society. Margaret Thatcher had transformed the way we live with her right to buy and a new building boom was under way. Though I did not realise it at the time, the who, the what, the where, the why, and the when, of my architectural career, was destined to finish in local government. This was just as well, for the post carried a contributory pension scheme, something which I had never given a thought to before. How many of us do in earlier years. When we are young we are more inclined to live now and pay later rather than pay now and live later.
When I secured a temporary post with Solihull Borough Council to supervise the erection of a new community centre in Shirley, I was offered living accommodation in an unfurnished empty one bed flat on the14th floor of a block of council flats in Chelmsley Wood. A suburb which was closer to Birmingham International Airport, the railway station and the National Exhibition Centre than Solihull itself. For many weeks, at weekends in a strange ritual, I came home with an empty car and returned with a car full of furniture. Bed and bedding, tables and chairs, pots and pans, toiletries and towels, they all found their way down the M1. Twenty eight flights of stairs was a daunting prospect when the lift wasn't working, but they were even more daunting in the early hours of a Monday morning when I carried furniture up them. Being housed not far from the N E C did have it's advantages though. I was probably the only person ever to walk to the motor show and back when it was held there that year.
On impulse I took a St John's ambulance First aid course in what spare time I had, but having passed the qualifying examination after the intensive eight week course, I dreaded the thought of someone enquiring if there was anyone around with a knowledge of first aid at the scene of some accident. For some time I lived in constant apprehension of being called upon to attend some emergency or other and actually having to do the things which I had

been trained to do. I tried to console myself with the thought that such things are probably unbearable until you have them to bear, but since no one has ever asked, I have never found out

With Caroline and Christopher old enough to look after themselves, June joined me when the post was made permanent. We bought a house in Balsall Common, an attractive leafy village about five miles from Solihull, where she took a clerical job in the local pub to pay for a few luxuries whilst I continued my supervisory work to pay the mortgage. When I took the opportunity to revisit many of the places I had known as a child during the war years, I found that they all looked pretty much the same. Warwick, Leamington Spa, Kenilworth and Stratford, had largely escaped the holocaust that had been brought down on nearby Coventry. Unlike this city, which had been largely rebuilt in the insensitive concrete vogue of the sixties, they still retained their original layout and characteristic buildings. With the completion of the community centre in Shirley came my first, and probably my last, opportunity to meet royalty.
It was the year when the Royal families television appearance on 'It's A Knock Out', proved to be the start of the slow decline in their esteem. The centre was to be officially opened by no less a personage than Her Royal Highness, The Princess Anne. Since I had been so closely connected with the new building, I received an official invitation to the opening ceremony together with some instructions on royal protocol. What to wear, how to stand and how to bow, what to say, and what not to say in the unlikely event of her striking up a conversation with me. It all sounded a bit daunting, but in the event it proved to be something of a non event. I saw her at close quarters, but I was never introduced. Her programme was apparently running late. After a somewhat shortened version of the opening ceremony and a quick visit to the royal powder room, which had been specially provided for her visit, she left early with her entourage in the general direction of Birmingham airport. I was a little disappointed that I never did get to shake the royal white gloved hand. There had been a great deal of publicity in the local press concerning the event, and given the opportunity, I might have disclosed the contents of a time capsule that was buried in a very secret location, known only to the readers of the 'Solihull Times', the 'Solihull News', the 'Birmingham Evening Post'......

As much as we enjoyed living in the West Midlands we still felt strong ties to the North East. That was where our families and our children were. The journeys back down the M1 to visit them were becoming increasingly tiresome, and I believe we both felt that, like the Jedi, one day we would return. When the opportunity came to move back to our routes it was too

good to miss. The article appeared in one of the Architectural magazines. Hartlepool Borough Council required a Principal Architect. I found myself in the right place at the right time, when shortly after taking up my new post, my new employers won 'City Challenge' funding to develop and upgrade the fabric of the town. It provided the newly appointed young forward looking Chief Architect the opportunity to revitalise and haul the Architectural Department into the computer age, and gave me the satisfaction of finishing my career designing some choice buildings.
That satisfaction however was tempered with some degree of frustration. If the eighties had seen the introduction and popularity of the personal computer into the home, then the nineties had witnessed the introduction of computer aided design into the office. What we have to learn to do we learn by doing, but I had great difficulty in learning how to do it. Old habits die hard. Ironically enough the younger generation in the office had the computer skills but lacked the design and construction experience, whilst I had the design and construction experience and lacked the computer skills. All in all I found the new medium somewhat of a frustration - as many of my generation do. I often found myself having to ask for advice and instructions to complete something on my computer which I could have done far more easily, and much more quickly, on a conventional drawing board.

When the lottery was introduced in the mid nineties, it helped to fund many of the good causes and charity applications that had been put on hold by the council, but how ironic it is that the lottery tickets are bought largely by those in our society who can least afford to buy them. Why does the Government allow the unaccountable members of the misguided Community Fund to spend such huge sums of money on unnecessary teams of administrators and all manner of spurious causes. Why does it allow them to squander so much on anti-British organisations and other controversial issues contrary to our national interest I wonder. I can think of a few war veterans and Servicemen's charities who would benefit. No lifeline for them though. Are our own people and their worthy causes not worthy enough. They don't appear to be.

I came to writing quite literally by accident. What I saw as an embarrassment when I damaged my achilles heel during a game of five-a-side football shortly before I retired, and what the doctor thought as foolish, June saw as an opportunity. 'You can't do a lot on crutches. Why don't you start writing that book about your experiences on Christmas Island that you're always saying you want to write about'. It sounded like good advice. There were things I wished to say, in a way I wished to say them, about the use - or misuse - of servicemen during the British nuclear testing programme

on Christmas Island in the late fifties. Acting on her prompting, I took my first hesitant steps into a career which I knew nothing about.
Like the inventor who has to pay to put his idea into practice after his patent is granted, I soon discovered that the first time writer has invariably have to pay a 'vanity publisher' to have his book published after writing it. Aspiring authors beware. It is a cruel thing to say, but you have to ask yourself who is going to read me anyway. It is easy to get excited when family and friends sing your praises and such a publisher appears enthusiastic about your work, but many are far more concerned about the cash they require in advance than the later promotion of either your book or your interests. There are a few good vanity publishers about, but many more have problems with their printers and distributors, others have cash flow problems, and some go into liquidation. It seems that the great majority of first time authors can be assured of three things. The book won't sell, it won't make a profit, and the high street bookshops won't stock it.

Authorship does however open a few doors which for other achievements might surprisingly remain closed. A month or so after publication of my first book and a year into my retirement, I was asked to appear on the Alan Wright Show on BBC Radio Cleveland to talk about it.
I had never been on the radio before, and the hour long programme looked an intimidating prospect. I felt extremely nervous on the day, and the situation wasn't helped when I arrived at the studio a half hour or so before the broadcast, to hear Alan repeatedly telling his listeners how extremely interested they would all be in his next guest, 'what an unusual story he has to tell....' It didn't help. 'Forget the microphone, just imagine we are chatting over a glass of beer in the pub', he said by way of encouragement only minutes before we were due on air, 'you'll wish it had gone on longer when you finish'. At that moment I wished it had finished long ago.
During the programme I had to chose four records representative of four stages of my life. The theme music from 'Dick Barton, Special Agent' - not forgetting Snowy and Jock - seemed to best typify my childhood days, whilst Glen Miller's 'Tuxedo Junction' seemed more appropriate to my Youth - The big band era. A time of record players and Bush radios, of 78 records on 'His Master's Voice', 'Brunswick' and 'Columbia' labels which scratched and broke so easily, and sapphire gramophone needles which, it was claimed, 'played 5,000 times without replacement'. Romance was a difficult choice but I recalled the year I spent on Christmas Island during my National service where, in company with other young men long since separated from wives and girlfriends, I listened to the crackling sound of the Everly Brothers singing 'All I Have To Do Is Dream' on our small portable radio. It was broadcast from Honolulu on Radio CIBS on Lazy Sunday afternoons when I

learned that absence does indeed make the heart grow fonder. Funeral theme music was an even more difficult choice, but I settled for the theme music from the film '2001', by Richard Strauss. In a year when the Super powers signed an historic arms treaty, I think my choice was something to do with floating in space and suspended in time, to see just how this planet of ours has shaped up to it's problems by the year 3001. My generation won't be around then of course, but for those who are, watch this space....

# 12. HESITANT STEPS

*I have few qualms about flying. Must be something to do with being cocooned in the confines of a tube and the inability to relate to the ground so far below. Travelling in an aircraft is one thing, but looking down from high buildings - particularly those in the course of construction - is something else. This short story, though a fictitious one, is typical of the many situations which people with the same irrational anxiety as myself occasionally find themselves in during the course of their careers.*

The sound of heavy rain drumming on the bedroom window and the noise of the probing wind in the guttering, finally roused him from a fitful sleep. Glancing at the bedside clock, he noted that it was only three-o-clock in the morning. He had been dreaming again. One of those restless frustrating dreams when he found himself struggling to climb an endless ladder without ever reaching the top. Gently half raising himself on his crumpled pillow, he found himself thinking over what he had to do later that day. A building contractor was awaiting his approval of the external cladding of a multi storey building he had designed, and he would need to inspect this from a forest of scaffolding and ladders that still surrounded the structure. What would be a routine inspection for most would be somewhat of a trial for him. He had always had an irrational fear of heights and, in the all consuming darkness and silence of that unreasonable hour when resistance is at it's lowest, he found it difficult to rationalise his thoughts.

Going up and coming down a ladder from even a modest height had always been a problem for him. He recalled the many occasions in his long career, when he had been called upon to inspect some fault or defect on a building at high level, and which had invariably involved the use of a portable framework of some description. Once up, he had spent a good deal of the time he should have spent examining the problem, wondering how difficult it would be to get down again. The ladder always seemed to be too vertical or far too short, barely projecting above the edge of the roof, scarcely long enough for it's purpose. Why wasn't it fixed at the top he often wondered, and where was the guy who was supposed to be holding it secure at the bottom. It was that first hesitant backward step into space that worried him, and afterwards the ominous sway halfway down.

If it was a phobia he hadn't mentioned his aversion to anyone. On site he was invariably surrounded by gutsy tradesmen and site foremen who had spent most of their working lives working at great heights from scaffolding. They expected the same cavalier approach to clear vertical space as themselves. To aid his efforts, he remembered that the contractor had thoughtfully promised to remove the protective cocoon of hessian surrounding the scaffolding and ladders to provide more light for his inspection. Ironically now, from the top of the structure, it would be possible to look vertically down a clear seven storeys. He tried not to think about it. He tried to make his mind a blank. After all he reasoned, if he failed to get any sleep that night, he would surely feel the worse and less able to deal with his dilemma in the morning. The logic was right but it did little for his slumber.

The rain had stopped and the wind had abated a little when he made his way to his firm's offices later that morning. No chance of a delay due to bad weather then. The thought had earlier crossed his mind.
'The boss wants to see you first thing', a colleague announced when he arrived. Such remarks always sounded ominous first thing of a morning, but on occasion they can be the harbinger of good news.
'I've just had a phone call', the Partner declared when he entered his office. 'It seems we have a problem with the Market Building project. I'm not sure what it is, but it sounds important. Can you go and sort it out straight away. I know you had arranged to inspect the cladding on your College project, but I will ask someone else to do it. Is that Ok with you'.
It certainly was. What a relief he thought. It was obvious of course why he had been asked to go. He had prepared the drawings of the Market building himself only a few years previously, and the building was coming to the end of it's defects liability period. During the half hour or so it took him to drive to the site he pondered on what the problem could possibly be. Maybe it was those troublesome finishes on the ground floor again.

When he arrived at the site, he was met by a concerned looking Market Hall manager.
'Thank you for coming so quickly', he announced, 'We appear to have a problem with the higher level roof which has developed a rather nasty leak. It may be due to the heavy rain we had last night. I know you'll want to take a look straight away. I've managed to get hold of a long ladder for access. It just about reaches the parapet. I think you'll manage. Do you want me to hold it at the bottom. Mind you don't slip......

# 13. A BARRAGE OF DRIVEN SAND

*The wind blown sand on an English beach can be a real nuisance, but the sand storm I experienced whilst working in the Middle East was something quite different. On that memorable day the strong wind that whipped up six foot high walls of sand around the villa that served as our office was completely unexpected.*

❖

Sunday, 26th August 1976

There had been a certain predictability about the weather since our arrival earlier in the year. In the hundred plus degree of heat, day had followed day, with little or no change other than the inexorable progress of the sun across a clear azure blue sky. When the gale force wind arrived without any warning around noon, the blown sand and grit that came with it seemed to find it's way into the villa through every nook and cranny.

You have to bend with the wind or break. Any plans we may have made for survey work outside were quickly shelved when we watched local mini twisters gather up the surrounding scattered debris of recent building work, before spiralling it up into the air and hurling it against the walls of the surrounding villas. With sea and sand lost to view through the windows of our own villa in the maelstrom, the eerie irregular whine of the gale force wind drowned the familiar hum of the air conditioners, and the insect screens covering the windows were subjected to a shower of missiles in a barrage of driven sand.
Few of the exposed lights on top of the decorative site boundary walls survived the continuous onslaught of blown packing cases, pieces of wood and small stones, and they were picked off one by one to the sound of shattering glass. At the height of the disturbance, with the squeaking entrance gate swinging wildly on it's hinges, our recently erected sign board was torn from it's roof fixings and came crashing down to break the recently laid tiles on the front terrace.
Shortly afterwards, with the immigrant workforce sheltering inside, some unfinished walling and partly cured concrete balconies of an adjoining villa fell to the ground in a heap of debris when the makeshift supporting scaffolding and formwork suddenly collapsed in a pile of timber props and boarding, leaving the remainder of the structure to the mercy of the relentless probing wind. In our own villa, a large amount of sand suddenly

cascaded down the stairway when the door giving access to the flat roof was forced open by the strength of the wind.
'You did close the car windows didn't you'. The thought was on both our minds. When I reluctantly hurried outside to check, I found it was difficult to breathe in the suffocating wind driven sand and grit which clothed my hair and stung my uncovered arms and face like hundreds of tiny needles. Through half closed eyes I saw that we had made the car secure, but how ironic I thought. After the recent thorough clean in the Dubai garage with a water hose, the car, like everything else caught up in that turbulent confusion, was being subjected to a further clean by sand blasting.

The vast and timeless lunar like-desert, where temperatures cruelly burnt by day and indifferently chilled by night, had seen it all before. The wind blown drifting sand would be diminishing visibility, to the extent of making driving impossible on the blurred outline of the intrusive tarmac roads. The endless serried ranks of sun bleached sand dunes would be moving more quickly now. Always blown South East by the ever present North West wind, their sharp creamy tops would be rippling and curling over like the crest of a wave, marching relentlessly on over the hard desert floor, choking the rare desert wells, filling the wadis and covering the tracks of man, camel, and vehicle alike. Deep and swamping, one step up and a half step down, they were difficult to clamber up at the best of times. They would be impossible to climb now.

The wind persisted throughout the afternoon, then surprisingly abated as quickly as it had burst upon us. Horizons were restored. Sea and distant road became visible once again, and the inquisitive roaming black goats re-appeared to consume anything remotely edible. All around us the damage was inspected as clearing up operations began to the now familiar shouting of instructions in Hindi and Pakistani. In the distance I heard the sound of the holy men calling the faithful to early evening prayer, and as I dug out one side of the car from the drifted sand in the fast fading light, I thought I heard Graham shouting from the kitchen. 'I think our dinner is going to be a bit gritty tonight'.

# 14. WALKING INTO ANOTHER WORLD

*When I accepted a position in Qatar with an established Architectural practice in the early eighties, little did I realise that I would be privileged to become one of the few, possibly the only, male ever to set foot inside the majlis (teachers rest room) of a girl's preparatory school during school hours. In this Islamic culture of strict segregation of male and female, this most private and secluded part of a girl's school was strictly forbidden to males - even to the Minister of Education.*

*'If I had not seen it I would not have believed it', the Iraqui partner in the practice was moved to declare when I finally returned from that forbidden sanctum.*

*In this emerging country like many of those in other parts of the Middle East which were being catapulted into the twentieth century on a rising tide of oil sales, education for both boys and girls within the framework and teachings of Islam had been given a high priority. What after all could the wealth from the country's abundant supplies of the black liquid gold which had been laid down millions of years ago thousands of feet below the ground be better spent on the ruler believed.*

*My unusual circumstances had arisen as a result of the Qatar government's crash programme for building schools. Having completed the school buildings themselves and erected the high outer screening walls, the recreational space between the two had been left as a sea of sand and my project at the time had concerned the provision of sports and playground facilities to these outer areas. To accomplish this, it was necessary to visit a typical school of both sexes and meet with the teachers in order to establish a brief and agree proposals. Something that could be standardised and used as a model for all the boys and girls schools throughout the State.*

*As anticipated, the visit to a boys school had presented no problems at all. The visit to a girl's school however had taken a great deal of arranging but despite the concern of the police and many high ranking government officials, the unique situation and urgency of the matter was recognised and it was eventually agreed that someone from the practice had to go....*

❖

Wednesday, 17th October 1981

It was hot and humid on the morning of the meeting in the appointed school. At the main entrance of the nearby headquarters of the Mobile Police Force, where the national flag on a look out tower flew limply in the debilitating heat of mid morning, a uniformed policeman sweated out his duty in a solitary sentry box. Typical of all girl's schools it had high outer boundary walls, solid metal entrance gates, and a guards room, all designed to keep out unwanted visitors and away from prying eyes. When I left my entourage of security police and disbelieving Ministry officials at the school gates in company with the burly school guard, I felt hot and uncomfortable in the suit and tie I had decided to wear for the occasion. We had previously agreed that, despite the heat, the situation demanded something more formal than the more casual cotton slacks and open necked shirt that we normally wore.
Not knowing what to expect and feeling more than a little nervous at being the centre of so much attention, I was conducted across the sand beyond the boundary wall by the burly guard who led me to a heavy entrance door which gave access to the school buildings. Not surprisingly this was opened by an elderly woman traditionally covered by her 'abayah' (full length black garment to completely cover the head and body), and 'burqua' (black and shiny canvas mask to cover the eyebrows, nose and mouth). Following the anticipated greeting of 'As salaam alaykum' (Peace be upon you), and my now customary reply 'Wa alaykum as salaam' (And upon you be peace), I was beckoned in and conducted along a cool darkened corridor to the doors of the 'Majlis' (Lounge or meeting room), which was located in the very heart of the school complex. After a hesitant courtesy knock and a measured pause, the door to this inner sanctum was opened by a strikingly beautiful woman in Western dress, who it transpired, was the headmistress of the school and whose name was Fatima.

Since my arrival in the country a year or so earlier, I had learned that traditionally men and women do not socialise or eat together. Women had little or no opportunity to openly express their femininity. Many men here saw women only as a mother figure, and were opposed to them working in any occupations which would bring them in contact with men. In order to prevent the possibility of any casual sex or the potential for their exploitation, there was strictly no meeting of the sexes in public or outside of the family. I had been conditioned to the sight of the local womenfolk, young and old alike, dressed in their traditional drab black garb walking furtive like in the town. Sometimes they would walk abreast in twos and threes, and sometimes as families in line ahead, their looks and sexuality

shrouded in mystery as they routinely adjusted their headdress to ensure their faces were hidden to all but their husbands.
When I stepped into that bright air conditioned heavily perfumed room, where a dozen or so young teachers had gathered to meet this intruder, it seemed that I had walked into another world. It seemed that I had been taken back in time. To a prohibited place. To a former age of eunuchs and beautiful slave girls.

Some of them were seated in large plush comfortable arm chairs placed around the richly decorated walls, whilst others sat cross legged or knelt in perfect poise on the exotic rugs which partly covered the cool marble tiled floor. Gone was the traditional all consuming black and colourless black robes of the Islamic woman's outer garment. These young women wore the fashionable long patterned flowing dresses of radiant reds, greens, blues and yellows, with beautiful cotton and silverthread decorative designs which sparkled at the neck and wrists, and decorous garments which would have done credit to a more modest version of the Yves St Laurent Spring collection. Some had a light veiled headdress draped over their head and shoulders in a casual fashion which they instinctively used to half cover their faces from time to time, whilst others displayed long luxuriant shiny black tresses that perfectly framed and complimented the natural beauty of their dark complexions. Many wore gold and silver pendants and charming bracelets, and others had large decorative earrings which dangled as if in enticement. I could not help but notice that the long slender fingers of their perfectly manicured hands were complimented by a rich red nail varnish and an abundance of gold and silver rings.
Deprived as I had been of the sight, sound and scented smell of so many beautiful women for so long, I could be forgiven for believing I had entered some oriental harem. I was acutely aware that no man had set foot in this inner retreat in such circumstances before, and none were ever likely to again. When I was introduced to each of them in turn, I believe they were as surprised and intrigued to see me in such surroundings as I was to be in them.
In this culture, it was customary and regarded as being socially correct to serve drinks and exchange pleasantries before any discussion on matters of business could begin. Not knowing quite what to offer this European stranger by way of customary refreshment, but no doubt aware of the English fondness for chocolate and fizzy drinks, I was presented with a large box of Black Magic chocolates and a bottle of Coca-Cola, which were politely served on a silver tray. Later on I would be offered extremely hot sweet tea served in tiny cups, which were embarrassingly refilled again as soon as I had drained them, until I was amusingly informed that it was customary to

wriggle the cup to signal that a further refill by the over attendant server was not required.

After a polite and hesitant start, and flattered by their attentions, I soon accustomed myself to the strange situation I found myself in, and warmed to them as they did to me. News of my arrival must have travelled fast for, throughout the meeting, passing inquisitive giggling schoolgirls, there fresh young post-pubescent faces uncovered now in the confines and privacy of the school, were soon unashamedly glancing through the windows to catch a glimpse of this male interloper. Despite such innocent diversions, I soon discovered that Fatima spoke excellent English, and through her, I was able to convey my proposals for the outer recreation areas to the interested teachers without too much difficulty. Because a girl has dreamy eyes it does not follow that she is not wide awake. Attentive and anxious to learn, and aware that this would probably be the only meeting we would have, they carefully studied my sketches and enthusiastically plied me with questions through their interpreter the whole of the time.

We finished our meeting after an hour or so. With the Coca Cola long since consumed, and the top layer of the Black Magic minus a few choice chocolates, my limited knowledge of Arabic unfortunately limited my expression of gratitude for the kindness and consideration I had been shown. I had no way of conveying just how much I had valued such a remarkable encounter, and they must surely have considered our meeting to be without like or equal. When I shook their delicate hands in those very private quarters, the farewell was warm, friendly and understanding. I would like to have said more, but sadly enough a general 'Coolay zain and Shruck-ran' (Very good and thank you), accompanied by an all embracing sweep of the hand and a low bow, was all I could muster under the circumstances.

I still look back fondly on that meeting. An event frozen in time when time appeared to stand still. I consider it to have been a unique experience and a great privilege. When I recount the story to other Muslim men, they wrinkle their brows and I see a look of doubt creep across their faces....

*I recall with wonder the spectacular dawns and the striking sunsets. Qatar - Middle East 1980*

*The singular beauty of the endless wind sculptured desert sands. Qatar - Middle East 1980*

*June secured a full time job as a receptionist in a newly opened museum building.*
*Captain Cook Museum - Stewart Park, October 1978.*

*The Gilbertese Village - Christmas Island 1958.*
*The inhabitants were moved from the island for the duration of the nuclear weapon testing programme.*

*I found myself in the right place at the right time when Hartlepool Borough Council won 'City Challenge' funding to develop and upgrade the fabric of the town.*
*Sheltered housing accommodation at the Headlands.*

*The design office produced many fine models of future projects. This one for a five storey extension to the Sixth Form College of Further Education.*

*Five time a day The Holy Man called the faithful to prayer from the top of the minoret of the mosque. Qatar - Middle East 1980.*

*We spent a memorable holiday in what was once Cliff Richard's Villa...... Albufiera - Portugal 1992*

*The front garden of our house in Balsall Common was as impressive as any other after an unuaually heavy fall of snow that first winter. Janaury 1986.*

*The Metropolitan Borough has changed a great deal since I sketched this view of the High Street. Solihull 1986*

*One for the family album. June and I with Caroline and Christopher. June 1994.*

*The legend is true, we did return to the Eternal City shortly after my retirement. Trevi Fountain - Rome 1998.*

# 15. HOME IS WHERE THE HEART IS

*If family life was once the cornerstone of our society, then the family house was the bedrock upon which our society was built. A home is something to which we all aspire to, ideally with supportive neighbours who smile at you over the boundary fence but don't attempt to climb over it. For me it has always been somewhere to retreat to at the end of the day, somewhere to rest, somewhere where I could shut the front door on the rest of the world and it's problems. Like most ordinary folk, for better or for worse, I have resided in quite a few homes and shut a number of front doors on many problems over the years.*

❖

There was a time when an Englishman's home was his castle. A place to feel safe and grow up in. A place to seek solace with the family at times of adversity. A home without the need for security bolts and lighting, electronic alarm systems, double glazing, razor wire and guard dogs to protect it, and a home without the obligation of a security insurance value rated by post code. How lifestyles have changed. The rented terraced town houses of the twenties and thirties have long since given way to the detached property owning suburban culture of a growing middle class society which has brought it's own rewards, but sadly enough, it seems that the tragic breakdown of family life has also brought it's own problems.
I never did get to design and build my own house. Despite the public's general conception, and their glamorous portrayal on television, very few Architects do get to build their own homes. Few can afford to do so. Realistically their average earnings are below those of many other professions, and in a strange anomaly, whilst most Architects spend more money - their client's - than anyone else, they have all the usual financial concerns of a mortgage, car and family themselves. My own rise up the property ladder has hardly been one from log cabin to White House. Like many other Architect's houses my house is like many others.

I was born under Cancer, after the crab, the fourth sign of the zodiac, in the same year as Mikhail Gorbachev, the soviet leader, Rupert Murdoch, the Australian media tycoon, and James Cagney, the cinematic public enemy of his time. The same year that the monumental concrete statue of Christ the Redeemer was built high on a hilltop in Rio de Janeiro, and the year that the world's longest suspension bridge and the world's tallest building were opened in New York. Illustrious figures to live up to and record breaking structures to emulate. Figures I could never hope to live up to and structures I could never dream of emulating. It was also the year that Alka Seltzer launched it's alkaline cure for upset stomachs and hangovers, and like many other sufferers in the morning after the night before, there would be times when I would claim it to be one of the greatest medicinal cures of the century.

Immediate past events are often difficult to recall, but how strange it is that those long since past come so readily to mind. The small terraced house in Tavistock road where I was born, had a small front garden which I wasn't allowed to play in. When we bought a black spaniel dog, which we aptly named Pongo, it made such a mess in the larger back garden that I couldn't play there either. The house was decorated in dark browns and greens as was fashionable at the time and separated from the one next door by a darker narrow passage which gave access to the back. It was a place for my pals to gather in when it rained, and it was here that we would often try to impress one another, as young boys do, with fictitious stories about things we knew nothing about. At a time when the refrigerator was regarded as a luxury, the small dark pantry had a cold slab for keeping meat and dairy products cool. In the Summer months my mother covered them with a gauze to keep the flies off and hung sticky brown paper from the ceiling to catch them on. We had a coalhouse which as a toddler I liked to play in and an outside toilet that I never liked to use. When it froze up in winter nobody could use it anyway. Unlike our neighbours, we never had a 'best room'. All the household activities centred round the smaller room at the back of the house. It was here that we ate all our meals, listened to the wireless whilst sitting in front of the open fire, and entertained any visitors. Oddly enough the bay window to the larger front room had net curtains to keep out prying eyes, but I cannot recall it ever being furnished.

Weather permitting we played in the small park opposite, usually on the grassed areas which had notices telling everyone to keep of the grass. There were policemen on foot patrol in those days. We ran away at the sight of one and returned to play when they moved on. The park also had a large circular concrete area in the centre which was ideal for football and other games, until the war years when a circular water storage tank was built on it. The water tank was never used, and I cannot recall that the water in it ever being topped up. There were notices on the high brick retaining walls prohibiting the public from throwing anything into it, but when the tank was demolished the contractors found precious little water but just about everything else.

In an age when a chicken was a rare treat for Christmas dinner, and the weekly shopping at a supermarket in a covered shopping mall a future luxury, most everyday things could be obtained close to hand. I seem to recollect my mother forever calling to me from the front door to run some errand to the live-over shops in St Barnabas Road. Oddly enough their names still come to mind almost as readily as do their sights, sounds and smells. Curbisons, the general grocers with it's shiny menacing looking bacon slicer in one corner, Jephsons, the newsagent which always had a window filled with colourful fireworks on Guy Fawkes day, Forsters, the sweet shop which had a little bell on the entrance door, and Hursts, the chemist with it's characteristic clinical odour of medicine where you could buy Zubes and other make believe sweets during sweet rationing.

Around the time that athlete Jesse Owens dominated Berlin's Olympics games to confound Herr Hitler's theory that White was superior to black in world sport, I was confounded by his role in something the grown-ups referred to as the gathering storm. In the event, I came to my use of reason around the same time that Herr Hitler lost his, when he unleashed that storm and invaded Poland. As Winston Churchill had rightly prophesied, the Government's policy of appeasement had failed, but none us realised at the time just how many traumatic years would elapse before the storm abated and peace was restored.
If my sense of reason had arrived before the war started, then puberty followed before it ended. Like most of my generation I had little or no knowledge of sexual matters. My sex education, for the most part, was limited to what I could glean from the occasional photograph in Health And Efficiency magazines, depicting young ladies playing netball on a camp site in a state of undress. Unfortunately they invariably had their backs to the camera or their lower half was discreetly covered with foliage. I first regarded the equipment which came with my adolescence with some alarm, and somewhat of a guilty secret, but like all young boys reaching manhood, I very soon discovered it could also be very pleasurable - and on occasion somewhat embarrassing. Unlike today's teenagers however, I would have to wait some time before I could put my manhood to proper use. That fumbling encounter would be played out one Saturday night on a small settee, in the reddish glow of a two bar electric fire, in the house of a local girl I had met whilst working in Pontefract. Whilst it was obvious that she had more experience than I had in such matters, what I lacked in technique on the night I more than made up for in ardour. The years between may have been years of frustration, and sometimes what seemed like unrequited love, but they were also magical years of wonder, imagination and anticipation.
Young teenagers in today's society seem unable to control themselves properly. They regard sex as something to be readily obtained in the

sexual market place like any other market commodity. They do themselves no favours when they indulge in promiscuous sex so soon after their adolescence in the knowledge that there will be few in society to condemn it, many to condone it, and sadly some to actually encourage it. For many there is little dignity left in the act now. Sex and womanhood have become an item of commerce, and the exciting mystery surrounding the difference in the sexes evaporates as quickly as does their respect for one another.

In the late forties, at the time Thor Heyerdahl was making his extraordinary journey across the Pacific, we made a more modest one when we moved from Linthorpe to Acklam into a three bed semi-detached house. Completed just before the war it boasted such luxuries as coloured leaded lights, a covered porch and a terrazzo front step. It had bigger rooms, something much appreciated by my mother, and a much bigger garden, which was soon disliked by my father who never seemed to find the time to look after it. For some reason he built a garage for a car we did not have, and a kitchen extension which we didn't need. Only in later life did my parents agree that it was a move they should not have made and they were never really happy there.
I recall that a young couple occupied the other half of the semi. He was well built, muscular and outspoken, whilst she was tall and thin, and somewhat withdrawn. They must have slept in the opposing back bedroom to mine, for through the dividing wall on occasion, there would come the grunts, groans and cries of what I took to be from a woman in some distress. For some time I naively thought that she was being assaulted by her husband in some way, until it suddenly dawned on me that they were having sex. How wrong can you be. Suspicion is often the companion of mean souls.
This was the house from where, morning and afternoon, come rain or shine, I cycled to and from my first place of work in Albert Road. A time when cycling clips were a necessity and it was customary for men and women to wear hats, which in deference to their faith, were removed by the men in church. It was also a time when the Catholic church still forbade the eating of meat on a Fridays, and Catholics still routinely practised what was preached. On such days, on my way home at lunchtime, I usually called in at Rush's fish and chip shop in Roman Road, where I stood in a long snaking queue inside before giving my order for 'a fish and two penneth with scraps, twice please'. 'That'll be one and two luv'. Six pence in today's currency. Wow....

Middlesbrough was a different town then. A time when iron and steel were at the heart of it's growth. A time before many of the fine old buildings and

rows of original Victorian terraced houses laid out in the grid iron pattern which so characterised the town, were demolished to make way for the Cleveland Shopping Centre and a new road system to satisfy the demands of the new motoring public. A time before an unsightly rash of concrete office and shop developments changed it's heart - and the heart of many other town centres up and down the country in the sixties.
My father would be amazed at the changes in his home town now. A time before road traffic jams and pedestrianisation. He would recall the destruction of Dickson and Benson Department Store by a mysterious fire in 1942, and the extensive damage to the Middlesbrough Co-op Society building and the Leeds Hotel by Herman Goering's Luftwaffe during an air raid in the same year, but many other buildings, like the Gilkes Street baths, have long since gone. The Gaumont Cinema was closed to the public in 1964, a victim to the growing popularity of television and bingo, the Wesleyan Chapel is now the site of the British Home Stores, a new office block now stands on the site of the old Corporation Hotel, the Royal Exchange Building was demolished to make way for a new road system, and Ayresome Park is now relocated to The Riverside where the local football club hope to win their first silverware. He would no longer be able to have his favourite tipple in the Masham, the Shakespeare, or the Wellington, but some of the haunts of his younger days can still be found, and rightly so. The unique Transporter bridge is still operating and will celebrate it's 100th anniversary in 2011, the Town Hall which celebrated it's 100th anniversary back in 1989, the Cenotaph unveiled symbolically on 11th November in 1922, and Albert Park, a rural swathe in an urban landscape, as popular now as it was when it was first laid out.

Perhaps not surprisingly we moved again in the early fifties to another semi detached house. A house built by a contractor who had acquired some prime sites in Acklam road, at a time when there was a great demand for new housing of the type he was building on prime sites. There is a tide in the affairs of men which taken at the flood leads on to fame and fortune. My father might have made his own fortune when the contractor enquired if he had any money to put into his firm. He even suggested that dad mortgage the house we had just bought with a mortgage. In the event, encouraged by my mother who thought the venture far too risky, he decided to play it safe. Failure is more frequently from want of energy than from want of capital, and so it proved. The contractor eventually obtained the funding he required from someone else, and he and someone else went on to enjoy the prosperity he had forecast. I often reflect that had he pushed open that particular window of opportunity which had been left ajar for him, my own life might have been so very different. It's a sobering thought.
I think it was Dirk Bogarde, the film star and writer, who once compared life

to walking down a corridor with many doors. We opened one door sometimes without much thought, and sometimes after careful thought, but the door that we eventually opened determined our future. There was no going back after it had closed behind us, only forward into another corridor with many more doors....

The eventful fifties saw the end of fourteen years of food rationing and the beginning of the second Elizabethan age, when Elvis stormed the charts and Teddy Boys stormed the streets. A decade when coffee bars and juke boxes ruled OK. I bought my first car second hand from a friend who lived over the road shortly after we moved. A Ford 'Consul' which, with the 'Zephyr' and the 'Zodiac', was one of the 'Three graces', a new innovative range of slab sided two tone cars which Ford had recently introduced, which went on to revolutionise the motor trade. We also acquired our first television set. Televisions, like fish fingers, were just coming on to the market, and we acquired our own set in time to watch all the pomp and circumstance of the coronation in black and white on the BBC channel, which was the only television channel it was possible to watch it on anyway.
In the year that Winston Churchill quit as British Prime Minister because of ill health, I quit my job with John Poulson because of his contrary attitude, and in the year that the Hollywood actress married playright Arthur Miller in a blaze of publicity, June and I were quietly engaged. Shortly afterwards I took the first steps to qualification as an Architect by passing my Intermediate examination, and shortly after that, I was called up for my National service. It would be two years before I could pick up the threads of my life again.

Born to late to see active service in the second world war, 375 young National Servicemen were born earlier enough to be tragically killed after it in Aden and Malaya, and fighting the North Koreans in Korea in 1950, the Mau-Mau in Kenya in 1952, the EOKA terrorists in Cyprus in 1955, and the Egyptians during the occupation of the Suez crisis in 1956. Had I not been deferred I may well have been involved in any of those actions, and under such circumstances I have often speculated on how well, or otherwise, I might have coped. Courage or the lack of it. True grit as John Wayne called it. In times of peace few of us discover the true measure of ourselves.
In the event, my National Service proved to be entirely different, and quite unique. After spending a half of it in the comparative comfort of Army barracks in Germany, I was destined to spend the other half in company with countless other young National Servicemen, in harsh conditions, on an Island on the other side of the world, fighting an unseen enemy and, surprisingly, write my first book about it. Sadly, for many of my fellow

servicemen, that Island would prove to be the wrong place at the wrong time. The Ministry of Defence has a lot to answer for.

After we were married June and I moved into a new bungalow in Acklam,after reluctantly selling the Ford Consul to put a down payment on it. We spent most of the swinging sixties in that dwelling, and did most of our swinging on a Saturday night on the dance floor with our friends and neighbours, to Alan Waller's band who played at the Ladle Hotel in Ladgate Lane. There were however other diversions.
After some success in a local competition, the Regional branch of the RIBA awarded me an all expenses paid two week study trip to Rome over Easter. June was allowed to accompany me and she proved to be the only woman in the party. The news that we had only recently been married must have preceded us for, in true Italian fashion, when we arrived at the small family run hotel we discovered that we were the only members of our party to be allocated our own room with a large double bed. It was all so embarrassing, but as the ancient saying goes, 'cor tibi magis pandit'. Roma had indeed opened it's heart to us in a most unexpected way. During our two week stay, I discovered the highlights of the eternal city and sketched the three thousand years of glory that was Rome, June found that shoes with stiletto heels were not the best of footwear for negotiating it's narrow cobbled streets and tiny piazzas, and we both learned that Italians eat a lot of spaghetti dishes, seemingly at every meal. With our knowledge of Italian limited to 'Scousi' (Excuse me), and 'Non capisco' (I do not understand), we saw a noisy English film dubbed in Italian at a local cinema where we found it difficult to follow the plot, and played a noisier game with horseshoes in a local park where we found it difficult to follow the rules. We were not notable enough to receive a papal audience, but on Easter day itself, we did receive the pope's Easter blessing. A distant, but familiar white shrouded figure, high on a balcony on the West front of St Peter's Basilica, he made his moving customary sign of the cross over the heads of the hushed crowds gathered in the huge Entrance Piazza, 'Pater et Filio et Spirituo Sancto....' We had seen the emotional ceremony on television in the past, and we would see it on television again in the future, but sadly enough, it seems that his annual message of peace on earth goes largely unheeded by fewer men of goodwill with each year that passes.
In the hope of returning one day, we threw a coin into the Trevi fountain before we bade Rome 'arriverderci. The legend is true. We did return shortly after my retirement to find that little had changed. Rome is still very much like an outdoor museum. The historical exhibits on the seven hills are still there. The new has been built around the old but the eternal city unlike life is truly eternal.

My daughter Caroline and younger son Christopher were born whilst we were in residence here. The former at Ardencaple Nursing Home in Middlesbrough, and the latter in St Mary's hospital in Newcastle. She accepts her locality but he claims to be a Geordie. The nursing home has long since gone, and the hospital, like most NHS hospitals, plagued as they are with superbugs and devoid of Matrons with their Matronly ways, is probably not as clean or as conducive to good health as it was then, nor as violent in the Accident and Emergency ward after eleven-o-clock on a Saturday night as it probably is now. By strange coincidence, Christopher was born at the same time that I finished my week long final examination in Newcastle, so two of us left home and three of us came back to make an ideal family of four.

We like to think that we are nearer God's heart in a garden. Perhaps that is why we spend so much time maintaining them. I laid out my second one when we moved to a house in Acklam in the late sixties, a time before paedophiles cruised the streets and surfed the internet, and made them essential for young children to play safely in. We moved in the same year that Richard Nixon moved in to the White House, and we moved out many years later in the same year that Ronald Reagan was re-elected to stay in it. It was the house where we first enjoyed the luxury of central heating, and the house where we first watched colour television at a time that many have come to regard as television's golden age. Fawlty Towers, The Good Life, Upstairs and downstairs, Abigail's party, The Ascent of Man, and Life On Earth. They were all great sitcoms, gripping dramas and innovative documentaries and, like the pop music of the time, as widely favoured and admired now, as they were then. I don't believe we shall ever see their like again.
We lived in Acklam throughout the troubled uncertain seventies. Through a decade which began with the West marvelling at the survival of the Apollo 13 crew after an explosion that left them adrift in space, continued with a spate of strikes and sex scandals, and ended with Britain adrift in a 'Winter of discontent', when a combination of a three day working week and untimely power cuts tragically put an end to the office games of five-a-side football. It was the house that the children grew up in. To be forever associated with school clothes, frilly knickers, tutus and cub uniforms, flared trousers, hot pants and sideburns. Of Christmas past when the grown ups still went to midnight mass, and the children played games with Wendy houses, Barbie dolls and action men. With space hoppers, skate boards and chopper bikes, pet rabbits, hamsters and guinea pigs. It was a time before convenience shopping replaced home made mince pies, and a time before we sat in front of the television all day, and judged how good a Christmas it had been on how

much we had enjoyed the Morecambe and Wise Christmas special. Sadly enough it was also the house we had to leave after I was made redundant. Just when you think you can make ends meet somebody moves the ends. In this case it was King Faisal when he imposed his oil embargo on the West, and threw the economy into recession. Though I did not know it at the time, my immediate future would rest on a tide of fortune and a time of change, and my experiences in a little known Emirate in the Middle East would be the subject of my second book.

In the early eighties following my return from the Middle East the economy had not fully recovered. While Carl Lewis was seizing Olympic gold in America I was seizing every opportunity to find work. Fortunately, I found a temporary post with the local authority in Solihull, where I took up residence in a small unfurnished single bedroom apartment in a block of council flats. June joined me when the post was made permanent, and we decided to sell the house when the children decided it was time to flee the nest. I know it was a difficult time for her. All mothers have a great sense of natural loss when their children first leave home. In her case, she also left behind her job, her family and her friends.
Life had come full circle for us as we watched our next home in Balsall Common near Solihull taking shape. We knew that a move from North to South would be more costly than a move from South to North, so we weren't surprised to discover that Solihull and it's suburbs was an expensive place to live. Our comparatively small dwelling looked even smaller when the foundations had been laid. They always do, but despite it's size, the house included an en-suite facility and boasted three toilets and I have to say neither we nor our visitors were ever caught short. If the house was small, the plot was big. The day we moved in I had doubts about ever completing the garden at the rear, and in the event I never did. Our stay in the West midlands proved to be short lived, and a short time after I had completed all the demanding preliminary work for the benefit of the next owner, we moved back to the North East to be near the family.

In the year that the new Pop superstars united to feed the world, we moved to a house in Yarm to unite the family again. Once a peaceful traffic free market town with more pigeons than cars, it's cobbled streets have sadly enough been submerged under such a tide of traffic, that it now seems there are more cars than pigeons. The town still holds it's annual three day fair though. Originally the first day was devoted to the sale of horses, the second to cattle, and the third to sheep, but now, the earthy smell of livestock and tanned leather has been replaced with the sickly aroma of hot dogs, fish and chips and diesel fuel, and three days of discordant music, multicoloured

flashing lights and white knuckle rides.
Over the years we resisted the salesmanship of the innumerable firms offering UPVc replacements, but eventually succumbed when we joined the conservatory set, to discover that our extension was uncomfortably hot in the Summer and woefully cold in the Winter, and the ideal place for Miaow the family cat, to snooze away the Spring and the Autumn.
This is the house we made our final mortgage payment on and the house I retired into. The house where I adjusted my alarm clock to a lie in mode and my body clock to a laid back lifestyle. I have my own study now. A converted third bedroom. Somewhere to retreat to on washdays, at the sound of the hoover, or when I feel I'm not wanted. It's unkempt and untidy, and it gets very dusty, and June just shuts the door on it, but it's a place where I can do my own thing in my own little world. Every man should have one. This is where I did my drawing before I retired and where I do my writing now before being informed that dinner's ready. A place where I can reflect on the past - and a place where I can hoard all the things that I know would otherwise be thrown out.

We all have our strengths and we all have our weaknesses. I had been very fortunate to have gone through life without any major injury, but in the year that Tony Blair realised his dream of becoming leader of the Labour Party, it was here that I first realised just how much we take the simple things in life for granted. My own achilles heel proved to be my achilles tendon which consigned me to crutches for three weeks after an injury playing a strenuous game of five-a-side football. Will I ever play the violin again I mused, as I hobbled self-consciously along the High street, whilst secretly envying those who could walk unconsciously down it. How I envied their mobility. Did they realise how lucky they are I wondered. How sad it is that we fail to appreciate the more mundane things in life. How ignorant we are of our bodies. How oblivious we are of our ability to function, and how blind we are to our general health and our well being, often until it is too late. If time wounds all heels, it also it also heals all wounds, but typically enough, once I was mobile again I soon forgot both the affliction which had so restricted my life, and the circumstances that had caused it.

Home is where the heart is, and for my generation there was less uncertainty about acquiring a mortgage for a home to put your heart in. International matters have always governed the economy, and bank rates will always determine mortgage rates, but we were never tempted by advisers miss-selling endowment schemes which gambled on the stock market, neither were we plunged into negative equity because of the uncertainty of it. There have always been economic cycles, but we rarely talked about housing booms, second mortgages or mortgage shortfalls. Given the temptation of obtaining ready cash on the paper value of their property now, I wonder how many will ever own their own home in the future. It seems moreover, that many couples discover that they do not wish to live together anyway. In our materialistic society where divorce and remarriage are commonplace, families break up and young couples delay having children, or decide to have no children at all, maybe we are witnessing the demise of the traditional family home with a two parent family - and the stability that goes with it. Perhaps the traditional two up and two down, will now be replaced with a new one up and one down to satisfy the demands of those who wish to live alone in the choking brown land of the inner cities, or on the ever decreasing wedge of green belt. Either way, the omens are not good.

# 16. REPLACING THE ADAPTABLE CAMEL

*To the average Westerner the camel is of no more interest than an animal to be seen in the often cruel confines of a zoo. To the nomadic Arab tribesman of the deserts however the camel was, and in some parts still is, the reason for his existence. Without the camel there would have been no Bedouin. Before the commercial export of oil and the impact of the internal combustion engine on desert life, the adaptable camel was the only available form of transport which allowed them to develop and maintain their nomadic lifestyle in an environment which cruelly burnt by day and indifferently chilled by night. Lawrence Of Arabia referred to them as 'ships of the desert' and his perceptive reference is not without foundation. Notwithstanding the introduction of modern technology into their world however, such is the long held respect of the camel that many Arabs in a life threatening situation in the desert would still place their reliance on the camel for survival. Like other expatriates in the Middle East a quarter of a century ago, I had to place my reliance on the motor car and come to terms with a markedly different set of values and a whole new range of driving conditions.*

❖

Since my retirement the arrival of the morning post has become something of an event. It may be the void after dealing with a lifetime of business correspondence, but the sound of the mail being pushed through the letter box still fills me with a sense of anticipation. At a time of life when I much prefer the streets to be aired before I venture outdoors, it has even been known to drag me from a warm bed on a cold winters morning. It's usually junk mail these days of course, but when a letter from the RAC arrived the other day enclosing my new membership card informing me that the coming year was surprisingly my twenty ninth year of membership, it set me thinking. Some serious thoughts initially. About my first car, my present car and how many cars, and then more frivolous ones concerning the number of miles I had driven, how many times I had been round the world, and howmany return trips to the moon I had made.

It also set me thinking about the most unusual places that I had found myself driving in over those years. Places that required a little more than the rudiments of the Highway Code. Negotiating the narrow tracks in the more remote parts of the Scottish islands with little more than the company of steaming long haired Highland cattle sprang to mind, as did driving in some parts of Europe overwhelmed with maps and paperwork. Driving in Hawaii, and on the newly laid roads of Christmas island at the time of the British nuclear testing programme were singular experiences, but on balance, I decided that none could really compare with the unique conditions of driving in the Middle East.

In the mid nineteen seventies, with the economy of the Western World in turmoil following King Faisal's momentous oil embargo, the Architectural firm that I worked for as a junior partner decided to set up a branch office in the Middle East. The venture was a gamble, but at the time it appeared to offer the best chance for the longer term survival chance of the practice. When we arrived in the remote Northerly Emirate of Ras al-Khaimah, an unlikely area of mountainous and coastal gravel terrain situated in the peninsular separating the Arabian Gulf from the Gulf Of Oman, we discovered that after thousands of years of privation and a nomadic lifestyle in a hostile climate, it's peoples were being catapulted into the twentieth century on a tide of commercial oil. As a means of transport, the intrusive tarmac road was replacing the indistinct desert track and the internal combustion engine was rapidly superseding the adaptable camel.

Early in our stay, more concerned with image than practicality, we acquired a large but impressive American Ford Plymouth. Roomy and comfortable as it was inside, it's low ground clearance made it completely unsuitable for negotiating many of the rock strewn unmade roads and the deep sand once off them. Like all cars in that part of the world where temperatures can soar to over a hundred and thirty degrees in the Summer months, the interior had a unique odour of burnt dust and upholstery. Other than a few gnarled fig trees and date palms there was little shade to be found outdoors. Such was the heat that, after parking in the sun for even a short while, many parts on the inside of the vehicle were far too hot to the touch, and we found it was necessary to start the engine, close the doors, and turn on the air conditioning for a time before it was cool enough to venture inside. It was also strangely deceptive. Cocooned in the air conditioned comfort of the car, the azure blue sky and turquoise waters of the Arabian Gulf breaking gently over a white sandy beach looked cool and inviting, but we knew that their appearance belied the reality.
Having an American car presented other problems. Service and repair work could only be carried out at the 'The American Automobile Establishment' in Dubai, a rapidly developing city reached only after a long journey on the recently completed road across the desert. It was here, in

that sumptuous marble floored showroom, that the nouveau rich Arab clientele could be found admiring the latest gleaming American dream machines, some of whom might buy the latest model Buick, Pontiac or Chevrolet as they would the cheap petrol to fill it's tank. For them it was more convenient to buy a new car than repair the one they had.

With a booming oil industry in the Emirates, and the largest oil field on earth next door in Saudi Arabia, there was no need to shop around for cheap fuel in this part of the world. There was no onerous excise duty or value added tax to pay. It was moreover dispensed by attendants at the petrol filling stations with a smile and a service that would flatter the best traditions of the AA or the RAC, but after my first visit I concluded that they were not the best places to linger at.
After giving the keys to a young Arab attendant on the forecourt, I sat in the comfort of the air conditioned car as he filled the tank literally to overflowing, whilst a second lifted the bonnet and checked the oil, and a third cleaned the windows. If I had requested the tyres to be checked I'm sure a fourth would have obliged. Whilst their attentiveness was welcome, the cigarette my key holder was smoking was less so. With petrol spilling on to the forecourt from the overfilled tank and the air heavy with petrol vapour, the situation had all the ingredients of a real life disaster to match that of the siege scene in Alfred Hitchcock's film 'The Birds'. Perversely, in a country built on sand, there was none available on the forecourt to cover the volatile liquid. When I pointed to the no smoking signs, my smiling attendants simply stretched out their hands palm upwards, and shrugged. 'Inshallah' (as God wills), one of them said. It was a word I would hear many times over the ensuing year.

'Inshallah', there may be a fire, accident or flood, and 'Inshallah', people may be killed or injured and may or may not escape, was still indicative of a belief that any event, or the consequences of it, would be God's will in accordance with Islamic law, and this religious conviction applied in no less a measure to driving.
Few locals had the equivalent of a UK driving licence. They gave themselves their own licence to drive. We had been given dire warnings about the shortcomings of some road users, and we were aware that everything had a price - even human life. Collisions, minor and otherwise, were commonplace. There was always the danger of colliding with a camel which had strayed onto the highway at night, when there would be little chance of survival. Being very large, long legged, and top heavy creatures, they were invariably thrown on to the passenger compartment crushing the occupants. There was just such an accident shortly after our arrival, when the grieving

deceased's family was obliged to pay a considerable amount of money to the dead camel's owner by way of compensation. We were also acutely aware that in this land of a different language and culture, where dead before sunset meant buried before sunrise, there would always be a number of nagging doubts and questions to cloud the prescription of any medical treatment that might be required following a more serious road accident. At the back of our minds there was always the thought that anything beyond the healing powers of the restricted first aid kit, which we always carried with us in the car, might best be left to the three great physicians, nature, time, and patience.

Driving in this emerging Arabic town, with it's sweet musky odour of perfume and oils, was all noise and confusion in a babble of local Arabic, Hindi, Urdu and Farsi, and any signs, roadwise or otherwise, were meaningless. All in all it was hot, dusty, and a hive of activity. A large variety of foreign cars and trucks hooted noisily as they struggled to avoid the deep ruts and potholes, and all around was the continual assertive hoot of car horns and the insistent ring of bicycle bells. The air was filled with a strange mixture of unfamiliar sounds as the monotonous melody of the high pitched Indian sitar and the wail of Arabic flutes and pipes competed with the strum of the Western electronic guitar. In the constant mayhem it was possible to park anywhere and everywhere, and all manner of vehicles spilled indiscriminately between half complete buildings and onto the packed sand which served as the pavement. With worry beads draped over their rear view mirror, Arabs and Indians drove their left hand drive vehicles on the deeply rutted potholed tracks in a similar laid back style. Right hand on the wheel and left hand hung out of the open driver's window, they gesticulated in a pleading manner, resignation or disgust, as best befitted the circumstances.
'No point in waiting for a number seven bus then', I remarked when I was first caught up in he confusion,
'You'll wait a long time', came the anticipated reply from my colleague.

We discovered that driving over a moonless desert under a cloak of darkness could be a disconcerting experience. Devoid as it was of any form of lighting, and with only a featureless open space on either side of the unmarked road, the illumination of the cone of headlights gave the mesmerising effect of driving through an endless tunnel or a dense forest of trees, and only the headlights of a rare oncoming vehicle would dispel the strange illusion. We soon discovered the necessity of always carrying a spare can of petrol and water with us at all times and, after first getting stuck in the deep sandy terrain, we quickly acquired some skills of driving in deep sand when we learned to avoid violent acceleration and not break suddenly, maintain a constant speed and keep turning the steering wheel. Driving in that part of the world did have it's lighter moments however - sometimes literally. On one occasion, after a spectacular early morning drive to the airport in Dubai, when the dawn had arrived as it always did, in the form of a fiery orange ball which rose dramatically over the rugged mountains which separated the country from Oman, we were obliged to stop at some solitary English style traffic lights which stood sentinel like at a road junction and which defiantly changed to red on our approach. At that immature hour, with no other traffic in sight at that lonely desert crossroads, and no discernible movement from horizon to horizon, we felt obliged to sit immobile in contemplative silence for three or four minutes until the lights changed to green.... It was a situation bordering on the farcical, and one which could only be found in a country well ahead of it's own development.

On our crowded little Island it is difficult to conceive of a major highway completely devoid of traffic. The M66 over the Pennines at dawn on New Year's day might come the closest to such a scenario. One such major road at the time was the only recently completed single carriageway of the trans-peninsular highway that snaked it's way over the six thousand feet high Hajar mountains that separated the East and West coasts of the peninsula and, more in a spirit of curiosity than exploration, a colleague and I decided that we would like to be amongst the first Europeans to motor across this natural barrier.
Close to the slopes of the jagged arid mountains, where a few stunted trees struggled for survival, the desert scrub petered out and the cream of the gravely sand changed to one of deep orange. Beyond the rising ground, the forbidding mountain road with it's spectacular canyons, deep gorges and teetering precipices, was an incredible engineering feat hewn largely out of solid rock. Winding up and down with hairpin bends turning back upon themselves, some in shadow and some in a shaft of bright sunlight, it twisted and climbed ever higher, passing towering rocky crags, rock strewn dry wadis, and the occasional plain stone mound that marked a burial site. Near the top of the final pass, where the air was cool and fresh, there was nothing to disturb the wild beauty and solitude of the place, but even here in this wilderness, at the side of the road, we saw evidence of the uncaring throw away culture of modern man. A crumpled plastic Coca Cola bottle, an empty corned beef tin, a half shredded tyre....
If our descent was no less stunning, then our return over those same mountains later that evening was even more so when, in spectacular contrast, the road was bathed in the white glow of a full moon. So close it seemed, so large and so clear at this altitude. It was almost possible to see

it's craters with the naked eye and I can still recall the exhilaration of the experience. To the peoples of this developing nation, the completion of the highway over a natural barrier that had existed for twenty million years, was as amazing a feat as the giant steps for mankind that Neil Armstrong had taken on it's surface only seven years previously.

In this newly emerging country there was little or no regard for safety measures. There was no concern for the convenience of drivers or the inhabitants during construction work on the incomplete urban road system. In their dark shadows the open service trenches looked deceptively deep and dangerous, and the piles of sand from their excavation spilled onto the road between unfinished kerbstones. Empty cable drums, broken pipes and discarded containers littered the uneven pavement slabs. To the side of some roads, telephone poles lay end to end in the sand like giant matchsticks, whilst on others, they stood sentinel like at the roadside, arms outstretched, patiently awaiting their looping connecting cables. There were no traffic cones, tapes or other markers to warn, direct or guide either pedestrian or driver through the maze. Each made their own perilous way through the confusion as best they could.

Winter rains are sporadic in that part of the world. They usually arrive in the form of violent storms when the entire annual rainfall might fall in one torrential downpour producing flash floods. It came as a complete surprise therefore when, driving back to our villa a little after dark one night after shopping at the souk (market), a few drops of rain fell to create little crater-like indents on the windscreen and dusty bonnet of the car.
Within seconds the drops had turned into a deluge and such was my astonishment that, for a short while, I struggled to remember where the switch to operate the long neglected windscreen wipers was located, which at their maximum speed were unable to cope with the ferocity of the downpour. With eyes straining through the rain streaked windows for any recognition of my surroundings, the novelty of the situation soon gave way to the reality of driving on incomplete roads without street lighting, and completely devoid of any cat's eyes, road markings or boundaries of any description. I was moreover acutely aware that in the absence of any footway or kerbstones, there was a nasty drop of two feet or more on to the sand at the edge of the unfinished road. Any misjudgement and the car would surely be a write -off. Under the circumstances, I was very relieved when I arrived at the familiar turn off to our villa where, perhaps not surprisingly, I found my colleagues busily engaged in mopping up floors.

The year that I spent in that far off land proved to be a memorable one, but despite my best intentions I never did get to return to Ras al-Khaimah. I have yet to meet anyone who has. I feel sure that the infrastructure will be in place now and the traffic lights at the junctions of the completed urban road system will continue to give the green light to steady progress, but my own recollections are of more adventurous motoring in the heat and dust of that emerging town of over a quarter of a century ago. Youth lives on hope, older age on memory, but such driving, like life, is a reckoning we cannot make twice over.

# 17. HIGHLAND FLING

*I had driven to the South coast on many occasions, but my long held enthusiasm for visiting the Scottish highlands had been further fuelled after seeing Billy Connolly's 'World tour of Scotland' on television when the unspoilt solitude and drama of the country caught my imagination. I reckoned mid May would be a good time to go. We would have to go by car of course. There was no rail service to the Western Highlands beyond Inverness. Two days to travel to the Northernmost point, two days to sightsee and two days to return, all before the tourists descended to disturb the tranquillity of the place. With the Winter snow still lingering in the corries, there would be a scenic beauty, freshness and invigoration in the Spring air, and the writer in me warmed to thoughts of painting the word pictures. Our venture North proved to be an unforgettable experience. Suffice to say that, despite it's being on mainland Britain, I have met few people, Scottish or otherwise, who have ever heard of Durness - and I have yet to meet anyone who has actually been there....*

'Not a good day to set out', June commented peering out of the car's rain streaked windows at the gathering mist somewhere near the Scottish border, 'if it stays like this we won't see any mountains. I think we must have picked the worst weekend of the year to travel'. Making slow progress behind a German touring coach in the cloying cloak, the only visible indication that we had arrived in Scotland that morning was a solitary roadside marker which loomed out of the gloom somewhere South of Jedburgh. When we crossed the Forth Road Bridge later that day, the tops of the twin towers and upper lengths of suspension cables were eerily lost in the lowering cloud which hung over the Firth Of Forth, giving a whole new meaning to sky hooks. On the adjoining Forth Railway Bridge, the latticework of steel appeared even more ghost like in the drizzle and gloom. Surely even Richard Hannay would have found it too perilous to take even one of his thirty nine steps in such conditions.

Having completed a half of our journey, and by way of a change, the mist had been replaced by torrential rain when we arrived at the small guest house in Pitlochry, and the sound of the rain drumming on the roof light was

the last thing we heard that night and the first thing we were aware of the following morning.
'Not a good day to see Scotland's scenery but it really does start here', our host somewhat sheepishly informed us over breakfast the following morning. A glance through the window at the continuing downpour however strongly suggested that unless the weather changed we were destined to have only a limited view of this through the arc of the car's windscreen wipers. True to form, the idyllic postcards that we sent home from Aviemore later that morning showing the Cairngorms in sharp outline against a clear blue sky, gave lie to the reality of their covering in the lowering cloud and mist at the time. If there was little traffic and few people beyond Inverness, there were even fewer beyond the once thriving fishing port of Ullapool where it's harbour would once have been full of Russian ships. These have now long since gone, but other vessels including the local ferry to stormy Stornaway in the Outer Hebrides still ply the waters of Loch Broom. Closer to our hotel in Northerly Scourie, the land was truly abandoned to the wildness of nature. In these more remote areas, the road skirted the boundaries of isolated crofts where we were obliged to slow down to cross cattle grids or avoid sheep and newly born bleating lambs which, oblivious to any danger and the biting wind and drizzle, spilled onto the unfenced road. At other times, between the snow depth location markers which stood sentinel like at the side of the road, steaming long haired highland cattle would suddenly loom through the mist to lift enquiring heads over wire pens and push inquisitive noses in our direction.

'Not a good day to go to cape Wrath', said our waitress over breakfast the following morning in a dining room memorable for it's austere finishes and a display cabinet housing a seventy year old bottle of locally distilled Scottish whisky valued at £1,000.
'Can't afford to buy it, and can't afford to drink it if you do', the only other occupant of the dining room voiced dryly.
When we commented how quiet it was for this time of the year and enquired just how lonely life could be in this corner of North West Sutherland in Winter, she told us that her husband drove a snow plough for much of that time and sometimes the only way for essential provisions to be supplied to the local crofters was by helicopter. As if to emphasize the point she informed us that the weather forecast was for a persistent cold Northerly wind and drizzle. It was all very daunting, but undeterred by the elements we had come this far and despite June's misgivings I was determined to go the extra mile. In a parody of Scott our hotel would be the base camp from which we would launch our attempt to reach the most northerly point of the mainland....

Later that morning, a few miles North of Scourie, a sign post informed us that the road ahead was not suitable for coaches or caravans and their were few passing places. For the following hour or so, with visibility in the cloaking mist and rain reduced to the next bend on the narrow winding road, we made our solitary snaking progress over a bleak looking landscape seemingly devoid of life between black jagged rocks and even blacker looking lochs. At times we could be forgiven for believing we were motoring on another planet.
'Not a place to have a breakdown', I observed giving voice to June's thoughts and recalling earlier comments about helicopters.
Closer to the coast the sky brightened a little, bringing a glint to the tops of the rocks in the barren landscape and a glisten to the pools of water in the road ahead. When we arrived at what I considered to be the Northerly enough location of Durness, we parked in splendid isolation on some shingle covered ground overlooking the beach, where a strong icy wind blowing straight from the Arctic covered the windscreen in a mixture of driving sleet and salty spray. In the distance, an angry Norwegian sea spilled against the base of a desolate looking promontory in a curling white foam as sea and sky merged together in a blurred murky grey horizon. I glanced at the milometer to discover that we were four hundred and twenty five miles from home. It seemed a lot more. In truth, given the nature of our surroundings, it was difficult to believe we were still on mainland Britain. We could have been in another part of the world.

There was little incentive to leave the comfort of the car. June sensibly decided to stay there, but warming to a sense of adventure I ventured out on to the deserted beach where the icy wind cut through my anorac and numbed my face. At the water's edge, with the dare of boyish enthusiasm, I reached my own most Northerly point when I ran to touch the outer side of a black rocky outcrop. I had intended to scratch my initials in that remote location but I was obliged to make a hasty retreat in the face of a large incoming wave.
The beach was not a place to linger at in such conditions. After thawing out in the car, and prompted by the thought of a sustaining hot drink, we ventured into the small wooden hut on the opposite side of the car park which passed as a cafe. It was dark and somewhat dank inside. The only heat appeared to come from a couple of gas fires which bubbled and spluttered in opposite corners of the room causing condensation to run down the inside of the window glass and form little pools on the sills. A few other brave - or foolhardy - souls, still wearing their sweaters and outer clothing, sat talking at wooden trestle tables in familiar pose, their hands clasped around cups of steaming mugs of tea or soup. A couple of seasoned walkers

wearing heavy climbing boots and sporting incongruous tyrolean hats, poured over a map of the area, their heavy rucksacks blocking the aisle between the tables. It was for them as it was for us, a port in a storm, and it was here that we learned, perhaps not surprisingly, that the boat to Cape Wrath had been cancelled due to bad weather.
'Not a good day to go to Cape Wrath then', I said to the girl behind the counter.
'Not many are', she countered.

Durness's real claim to fame was it's proximity to 'Smoo Cove', but it's attraction still did not tempt June from warmth of the car.
'You go and tell me about it afterwards', was all she would say.
After negotiating the steep wooden steps down to he bottom of the cliff face, the view into the large irregular black opening to the cave itself was dark and foreboding. Inside it was wet underfoot and water seeped from above in large droplets which were difficult to avoid. Over the centuries, a waterfall from the higher cliffs had broken through the roof and now spilled into a cauldron of a pool in it's dark mysterious interior with a frightening thunderous roar. This spectacular backdrop had been created naturally over countless years and man had enhanced nature's masterpiece with some stunning lighting effects only a few years previously. It was an eerie setting. A place for quiet contemplation and I was the only one around at the time to quietly contemplate. This underground cathedral had been created long before I arrived on earth, and would be here long after I had gone....
'I took a couple of photographs but I don't think they will do the place justice', I said when I returned to the car where we sat for some time listening to a programme from a local radio station about the origins of Scottish reel dancing, whilst dreamily watching rivulets of rainwater race each other down the windscreen. When we arrived back at our hotel later that afternoon the rain had stopped but it was still too cold to sit in the conservatory, so we went back to our room to lay under the warmth of the duvet and watch television until it was time for dinner. Later that evening mine host, who seemed to know about such things, announced that the barometer in the foyer was rising and better weather was on the way.

The following morning we woke to welcome bright sunshine. Encouraged by this change in the weather, and energised by our third fulsome breakfast of Scotch porridge oats - we had resisted the haggis, tattis and neeps the previous evening - we walked down a secluded grass covered path through the wooded grounds at the rear of the hotel to the shoreline of Badcall bay, which in stark contrast to the inclement conditions of the previous day, was the very epitome of peace and tranquillity. The lightest of breezes rustled the leaves of the trees that spilled down to the shoreline occasionally ruffling the still waters around the tiny gorse covered islands in the bay, where birds of prey majestically swooped and dived in their natural habitat. Was that an eagle, a hawk or a falcon, I mused. After all, Handa Island with it's formidable cliffs and stacks, and famous as a bird sanctuary, was only a few miles to the North. We sat in silence on a rustic bench seat for quite a while in quiet meditation, drinking in the view and enjoying the warmth of the sunshine. The magical spell was only broken when a solitary fishing boat towing a small rowboat hove into view. The 'phut phut' of it's engine echoed mutely across the bay as it moved effortlessly across the calm waters, causing an ever widening bow wave to brake gently on the pebbled shoreline in it's wake.

That afternoon we took the coast road to the small village of Lochinver. Once again this proved to be little more than a lonely single winding track with few passing places, but what a transformation now. Unlike the doomsday like scenario of the previous day, when little or nothing could be seen of sea or sky, we could admire the views of the indented rugged coastline with it's lonely inlets and deserted driftwood strewn sandy beaches. As we negotiated our slow solitary progress in this unspoilt remote place, where the now familiar sheep with their thick coats marked with identification dye were our only company, the newly erected telegraph poles carrying a single wire along one side of the track were the only evidence of communication between the occasional croft and cottage. When we arrived at our destination there were few people about. After visiting the pottery, where surprisingly we discovered that the clay to make a variety of chinaware came all the way by sea from Cornwall, we posted a card to ourselves through a letter flap in the front door of a closed grocers shop which was marked post office, and which we hoped was the letter box.
In the now warm and sunny day we motored on to Inverkirkaig, an even smaller collection of cottages a little further down the coast, where there was nobody about. Here the whitewashed stone walls and grey slate roofs blended perfectly into the staggered outcrops of rock, yellow gorse, and the rich green of the conifers on the lower slopes of the nearby mountains. We could have travelled on to see the waterfalls of Eas-coul-Aluin which were claimed to be the tallest in Britain, but such was the solitude and beauty of our surroundings, and armed as we were with camera, binoculars and sketch pad, we inadvertently stayed longer than we had intended.
To the occasional 'coo' of a dove through the open roof light, and with the late afternoon sun dancing between the high mountains and reflecting off small lochs, we made our leisurely way back to the hotel in Scourie chasing our own shadow on a road completely devoid of traffic. Such are the vagaries of

the British climate - and the warm ocean currents of the Gulf Stream - that only in this part of the world could such a beautiful warm day have followed one so cold and unsettled.
'You know', I ventured after driving in a long contemplative silence, 'maybe we have been very privileged to have seen the Highlands in the way we have. Yesterday and the day before were just as impressive in their dark dramatic way as today has been with it's scenic beauty'.

The following day when we passed over the Moray Forth again on our return journey to Pitlochry, the tops of the towers of the bridge stood out bright and clear against the warm blue sky. When we got to the other side a road sign beckoned us to the battlefield at Culloden. On impulse we decided to pay the monument a visit to find the audio visual account of the historic struggle was as impressive as the complex of new buildings that had been built to commemorate it. Later we walked on the gravel paths over the infamous sloping sodden moor between flags which marked the site of the short but bloody battle in 1746, where we brooded on the glorious defeat of Bonnie Prince Charlie's Highlanders, his escape with the help of Flora Macdonald, and the subsequent break up of the Highland clans.
Travelling further South later that sunlit evening the broad rolling greenery of Perthshire was a complete contrast to the wild Highlands of the day before. There was a hint of snow on the distant Cairngorms and a fragrance of freshly mown grass in the air. Whether it's scenic beauty was admired through the windows of a coach, or for the more adventurous from snow capped mountain tops or cable car, this was the area most visited by the tourist. We had sought a wilder, untamed and uninhabited part of Scotland, but it was here that the fairy tale castles, colourful exotic gardens, charming woollen mills, salmon fish farms and distilleries, where it was possible to sample the pure malt whisky, could be found. Ah, if only we had more time......

We stopped in Edinburgh for a few hours on the final leg of our journey home. When we took a stroll down Princess street we found that the bustle and noise of activity in the city was a strange intrusion into the previous days of unreal quiet and tranquillity. We had been plunged back into the real world. There would only be the photographs now to remind us of our memorable acquaintance with that untouched Northern land so beloved of Billy Connolly.
'The car's done well', June commented a few miles from home.
'Yes, nearly a thousand miles in six days', I replied, and then as an afterthought, 'and in all weathers'.
She didn't mention the driver but I took her silence in that regard to vouch

for an acceptable performance. When we arrived home later that day, tired but richer for our experience, we found a postcard on the doormat postmarked Lochinver. We had penned a simple message to ourselves. 'Welcome home from the Scottish highlands'.

# 18. PRAGUE, CITY OF SPIRES - A TASTE OF OLD BOHEMIA

*With the freedom that came with my first year of retirement - and the sense of urgency that came with it - I was captivated by the thought of visiting this city of fairytale domes, soaring spires and fanciful architecture, after it's earlier occupation by the Nazis and only recent emergence from behind the iron curtain. Occupied by the Germans from 1939 to 1945, and governed as a Peoples Republic under the Communists from 1948 until 1989, had the artistic and cultural life of the city returned after it's liberation from the servitude of those years I wondered. Any short holiday here would certainly be different. It would also be hectic, but it promised a taste of old Bohemia and a flavour of the old Hapsburg monarchy before commercialism took route and spoiled the illusion - or I lacked the energy to undertake such a venture.*

Flying somewhere over Northern Germany, in those early hours when Airlines are uncertain as to whether they should serve early morning breakfast or late evening dinner, we pondered on the wisdom of an earlier hasty decision to make a DIY three day visit to recently liberated Prague, but when we landed at the airport, any concern we may have had about entry formalities and transfer arrangements proved to be unfounded.
The duty customs officer took but a cursory glance at the bland unimpressive pale peach documents that now pass as British passports, and the young taxi driver who transferred us to our hotel knew exactly who we were and where to take us. He spoke little English, and the drive in those early hours to our final destination was memorable only for the speed which he drove through the suburbs of the city. When I asked him, more in hope than anticipation, if he had arranged to collect us again later that week at the pre-arranged hour for our return trip to the airport, he just waved his hand and drove off. In view of the hour it was not the time for speculation however. It had been a long day. After checking in, we collected our keys, somehow managed to fit both ourselves and our luggage into a strange gateless two person lift, and found our allocated room on the top floor where we went straight to bed. The unpacking could wait.

Day One

The day only dawns on those that are awake. The following morning we overslept and had little opportunity to sample the continental buffet breakfast. We had intended to make a leisurely start to the day, but the coach which was to take us on our prearranged tour of the city that first morning arrived before we had eaten our croissants. Under the circumstances there was little we could do but wrap them squirrel like in a table napkin for later consumption and leave in great haste.
Our first port of call was busy Wenceslas Square. Named after good King Wenceslas, we were surprised to learn that he had a brutal brother. There was certainly a flavour of the decadent in the art nouveau buildings there, but the wide tree lined avenue between them was filled with the local populace who were largely window shopping and enjoying the late Summer sunshine which spilled through the foliage, dappling the colourful restaurant awnings, street furniture and people alike. A little later in complete contrast we walked more solemnly through the narrow cobbled streets of the Jewish Quarter with it's Jewish ghetto. Preserved during the German occupation of the city on the orders of Hitler himself as a reminder of their intended extinction, our guide informed us over 77,000 Czech Jews were killed in the holocaust. There was little to remind the casual visitor of those terrible times but I was mindful of the visit I had made to Belsen in Northern Germany during my National Service. An instructors course which I had attended, and which had been held only a few miles from the site of the former concentration camp, had finished a day early and on impulse a few of us had decided to visit the memorial there. There were few people about, and under a lowering sky and in a misty drizzle, we had walked in sombre silence on the gravel paths between the numerous mounds of grass covered earth, each of which which marked the location of a mass grave. Each mound had a simple plaque with the words 'A Thousand People Lie Buried Here'. Just twelve years after the camp had been overrun by the Allied Forces there was an air of gloom and melancholy about the place; no birds, no bees, no flowers, no trees. It was as if nature was in mourning for the crimes that had been perpetrated there, and the experience had left us in a sober and questioning mood reflecting on man's inhumanity to man.

With little sense of time, the pace of the tour increased as our enthusiastic guide seemed intent on showing his entourage as much of his historical city as possible, whilst evading any questions of a political nature or anything concerning the recent past. We crossed over Charles Bridge to marvel at Prague Castle which was guarded by designer dressed soldiers, and originally covered it was claimed with gold leaf roofing, and wandered

through the three courtyards with their fairy tale palaces which housed precious paintings and fine glasswork by Bohemian artists, and where, perhaps not suprisingly, classical concerts featuring the works of Mozart, Beethoven, Vivaldi and other great composers were a regular midday feature. It had already been a long day when we stopped for but a short while to take some photographs of the extraordinary stained glass windows of the 14th century three spired neo-Gothic cathedral of St Vitus, and thankfully paused to admire the panoramic view across the Vitava river and the city itself from the Castle heights. Sustained only by the croissants we had fortunately brought along with us, the marathon tour ended somewhat abruptly, with little warning and without any break or refreshment, in the early afternoon under the 15th century astronomical clock in the bustling pedestrian only Old Town Square, where we discovered, somewhat disconcertingly, that we would not be returned to our hotel.
Oft expectation fails what most it promises. Any thoughts we may have cherished of a well earned rest sampling the local cuisine and watching the world go by from one of the many pavement cafes, were soon dashed when I discovered that, in the haste of our earlier departure, I had neglected to bring any maps or documentation with me. We had not the remotest idea of the location of our hotel, and even more disturbing, we had forgotten it's name.... By the time that particular dilemma had been solved we had little energy left to return to appreciate the floodlit peaks, towers and spires of the castle, preferring instead to end the day in a local bistro close to our hotel that we chanced upon which, to our delight, served a most delicious apple strudel.
It had been a tiring and somewhat confusing first day. Back in our hotel room, it seemed appropriate to end it watching a French film with Czechoslovakian sub titles on television.

Day Two

Whilst not the best address in this more residential part of the city, our typical small hotel with it's basic amenities was clean and comfortable without being pretentious. Not wishing another hasty breakfast, we had set our travel alarm for a respectable hour, but the rattle of milk bottles and the raising of the shutters on the windows of a shop opposite disturbed our deep slumber early the following morning.
When we left the hotel the warm sunshine of the previous day had been replaced with an irritating light drizzle. Wiser now from our experiences, we had armed ourselves with maps and directions - and a brochure of our hotel showing it's location. When we boarded one of the numerous trams that snake around the narrow streets of the old quarter, the broader avenues of

the new city, and over the eighteen bridges across the river which connects them, it was largely filled at this late morning hour with the more elderly inhabitants of the city dressed in dark sombre clothes. Each with their own thoughts, these resolute people gazed thoughtfully through the rain streaked windows, ruminating perhaps on past traumatic events and wondering at the many changes that had occurred since the countries recent liberation and it's formation as the Czech Republic.

After alighting and finding our way through the labyrinth of meandering medieval cobbled streets where the rich aroma of freshly ground coffee filled the air and quickened the senses, we emerged into the Old town Square which we had been unable to explore the previous day.
Prague was neither bombed nor was it shelled during the war, but many buildings there still symbolically bare the bullet holes of earlier wars and uprisings. Ironically, the tower of the Old Town Hall was largely destroyed during the liberation of Prague by the Soviet Union in 1945, but fortunately the15th century astronomical clock in which it is housed has been fully restored. Leaving my wife to look around the many market stalls, each with their quota of ceramic buttons for sale and covered now with a small brightly coloured awning to keep off the irritating drizzle, curiosity got the better of me and I found the energy to climb the narrow steps inside the tower and find my way on to the roof. It was all worth the effort. When I leaned out and over the parapet and looked down I was rewarded with the unusual sight of a sea of multicoloured umbrellas. They were held by the large crowd which had gathered to witness the ritual of the skeletons and religious figures that come to life and revolve around the timepiece when it strikes the hour.
There were any number of eating places in the area selling inexpensive and unsophisticated but wholesome food for those not too interested in counting calories. Not wishing to sample such traditional local dishes as pork, dumplings and stewed cabbage at that time of the day however, we had a snack at one of the McDonald restaurants that could be found in the city - we were informed that there was already a Tesco store there as well. The place was full of noisy teenage tourists of all nationalities, and such were our surroundings that we could be forgiven for believing we were back in our own capital city.
Revived and feeling more adventurous, we ventured on to the clean, swift and efficient Metro tube and after some confusion about our eventual destination, we found ourselves in Wenceslas Square again. It was here, under the statue of St Wenceslas, that the communists had held their celebrations and May day parades, and it was here, also amongst the buildings still pockmarked by the bullets and the machine guns of the Russian Red army tanks in1968, that freedom was eventually celebrated

in1989, ending the forty year old yoke of communism and heralding the beginning of a new democracy.

Given our short stay, our hastily drawn up itinerary gave little time for rest or recuperation. Earlier that day, for a very modest sum, we had obtained tickets for a Bohemian party night. An early return to our hotel allowed us just sufficient time for a wash and brush up before taking a taxi to one of the larger hotels which was hosting the event. With appetites sharpened by anticipation and McDonalds now a distant memory, we ordered the 'Ceska specialita' of schweinebraten, nach bauernart, knodel and sauerkraut quite blindly from the menu, only to discover interestingly enough, that it was the pork, dumplings and stewed cabbage we had declined earlier in the day. If this repast was simple but adequate, then the cabaret which followed it was unique, colourful and spectacular. Not quite sure what to provide as more cultural entertainment for visitors to this newly emerging country, the organisers had brought together a rich variety of talent. The brochure had promised 'the best of local cuisine', and 'an informal unique mosaic of classical ballet, black theatre, folk performance and traditional costume, featuring the leading artistes of the Czech ballet'.
Needless to say the evenings entertainment fully lived up to it's expectations. We had bought our tickets in great haste and with some reservations, but the most enjoyable of occasions are often those which are more spontaneous. Comfortably seated at our table drinking the local Pilsner beer so close to those gifted performers, we agreed that this was one of those occasions.

Day three

We had already discovered that the best way to see Prague is by walking. With no particular destination in mind but wearing more sensible shoes for it's cobbled streets, we ventured on to the Metro again to emerge this time a short distance from the Charles Bridge.
No trams ran across this older structure, though it was possible to see them crossing the bridges over the river on either side. After walking under the formidable looking 14th century Old-Town-Bridge tower at it's Eastern end, we stood under the gaze of the many ancient statues of saints which lined the sides and watched a variety of buskers and street artists, including a young man on stilts doing wonders with puppets and two younger women playing a Beethoven violin concerto. On the far side of the bridge a dark foreboding flight of steps beckoned us down to Kampa island where we pondered on what dark deeds may been carried out in it's dark narrow back streets which, like those in many other parts of Prague, had not changed for over two hundred years.

Our wanderings brought us to St Nicholas cathedral where we chanced upon a wedding in progress and, mingling with the excited wedding party that had gathered on the pavement outside, we were somehow swept inside the church. Like many of the churches in Prague, the outside held little guide to the lavish ornamentation of stucco walls, rich frescoes, sculptural decorations and gilded statues that could be found within, but with doors closed securely behind us, and feeling somewhat embarrassed, we were little aware of this. Under the circumstances we felt obliged to witness the wedding ceremony itself ,watched by a congregation wondering no doubt whether the improperly dressed strangers in their midst were for the bride or the groom....

Fortified by a glass of beer and a pork sandwich at a pavement cafe, we wandered into Golden lane, a narrow 16th century street lined for the most part with small shops, where we paused from time to time to admire the hand cut Bohemian lead crystal, exotic silver jewellery, original pattern china and Gianni Versace clothing. After austere communist rule, Prague it seemed was hell bent on catching up with the West. Anxious to see as much as we could in the short time that we had, we found our way back to Malostranske Square, an area rich in fine palaces which are now used as Embassies, and sat for a while among the statues in one of the many quiet gardens away from the noise and fumes of the heavy traffic. When we crossed over the Charles bridge again later that day, the setting sun of late Summer cast a warm glow over the city and we speculated on how impressive the rich varied roofscape might appear in Winter under a white cloak of snow.
With the need for an early start the following morning in mind, we deemed it prudent to settle for a leisurely dinner at the friendly bistro where we had been made so welcome that first night. The travel agent had claimed that we really needed a week to sample all that Prague could offer, but over our second helping of apple strudel we had seen much of what we had wished to see of 'Touristic Praha'. The lesser known Prague sites, the mineral springs, the exotic night clubs and the casinos which claimed to 'have it all', would have to await a future visit. After all, we had both rubbed the bronze cross at the centre of the Charles bridge which the locals believed guaranteed a return to the city.

The same young taxi driver who had picked us up at the airport proved as good as his wave of the hand when he collected us for our return to the airport the following morning, and as fast a driver when he returned us there. When we arrived home early the following day we found the postcard which we are in the habit of posting to ourselves when travelling abroad. Postmarked 'Praha', it had the picture of an astronomical clock on one side and we had penned a simple message to ourselves on the other. 'Know the true value of time, snatch, seize and enjoy every minute of it'.

# 19. NOW WE ARE SEVENTY

*I had my seventieth birthday the other day. The magical three score years and ten. A veritable milestone. A time for reflection and a time for looking backwards rather than looking forwards. Seventy candles are a lot to blow out and, as someone once remarked, you know when you are growing older when the candles cost more than the cake....*

◆

In that long gone more innocent world when A.A. Milne set down his reflections on his more tender years, it would have been time to contemplate the proverbial pipe and slippers. Though it has not come to that yet, I must confess to feeling somewhat morose on the day at the thought of such a venerable age. A week or so on though, I have come round to accepting the situation. I take some comfort from the fact that in the lottery of life, you are not necessarily as old as you look but rather as old as you feel, and perhaps more importantly, as others see you. I still don't really know why I was put here, but I think I now recognise who I am now.

I don't feel any pressure though. I have come out of the fast lane and abandoned the early morning rat race on the A19. In my more reflective moments I take some consolation from the fact that I don't need to prove myself any more, and can rest on whatever laurels my family and friends have bestowed on me over the years. For better or worse I have run my own individual marathon. I cannot turn the clock back now. The past is history. Any more macho displays or sporting prowess can be regarded as a bonus and all the more rewarding for the effort as I try to convince myself that what I might have lost in agility I may have gained in maturity.

Time and tide stops for no man. It is at once the most valuable and yet the most perishable of all our possessions, and I am convinced that it passes more quickly the older you get. There was a time during schooldays when there appeared to be no life beyond an hour of double maths on a Monday morning. The lesson stretched into infinity. It was a time of waiting and a time for wishing. For schooldays to end, to wear long trousers, to start work, to be twenty one, to unravel the mysteries of sex. After that there was never enough time. The family album tells it's own story but, like the player who struts and frets his but brief hour upon the stage, I like to look back on the comedy/tragedy of life in the fond belief that I did it my way.

Though life has come full circle for me now I like to think that the glass is not so much three quarters empty, but still a quarter full. Ironically time itself has become life's most precious commodity. I regularly try to convince myself that there are still a full sixty minutes to every hour and twenty four hours to each day, that a full week has passed since I last checked the football pools, a full year since I renewed the car tax, and the world cup really is contested every four years. I am more inclined to do things today that I would have previously put off until tomorrow as, like the ebbing tide, that most priceless of gifts continues to slip relentlessly away. There was a time when the birds and the bees, the flowers and the trees and the colours of the rainbow, were not macho enough to be recognised or appreciated and the true magic of the seasons passed largely unnoticed. Only now it seems does their passing bring it's own significance. Perhaps it is because there is a more distinct measure to their numbers now.

Winning the lottery would not change my life for the better now, and I strongly suspect it changes the life of most of those who do win it for the worse. I have learned that true happiness only comes from the simple things in life. The energy and drive which spurred me up the material ladder of success in earlier days, has been replaced by a maturity which has come to appreciate that only achievement gives real satisfaction, and the realisation that money can neither buy good health nor the years to enjoy it. I sometimes reflect on how short a time we are here, and how short a time we are here to appreciate all the privileges we have become so accustomed to. Unfortunately some never do and some never have a chance to do so.

It is sad that we have to grow old after a healthy active life. To slowly lose accustomed energy and vitality and become aware of a thickening waist, stiffening joints and receding hair line, and hair that seems to grow everywhere but on the head, but I console myself with the thought that whilst we may finish sans hair, sans teeth, sans everything, the only alternative is even less attractive.

Over the years I and my generation have been privileged to witness a great deal of change. Unfortunately not all of it for the good I fear. If Nostradamus has been proved right in the past we must hope that he is wrong about the future. I am an optimist by nature but looking into that future I do not like much of what I can foresee. The world is not a safe place now. Global unrest and global fear stalk a world where the sword is now mightier than the pen. It is perhaps non too surprising that the more pessimistic of my generation see a future clouded by shades of civil disobedience, debasing of the franchise, over regulation and over population, a breakdown of law and order and endemic corruption.

Prime Minister Harold McMillan was right all those years ago when he

declared that 'we had never had it so good'. As children of the war years, we owe our very existence to those of our fellow countrymen and women who fought and died in the second world war to give us all the benefits of fifty years of peace in our country for the first time in a century. Childhood for most was a golden age of happiness and innocence. I and my generation have surely lived through the very best of times in this once green and pleasant land. Like all those fortunate enough to be born in a country which boasts one of the world's highest living standards, I was already a winner by virtue of my birthplace and birthright. My generation has surely been born in the right place and lived at the right time. Life has never been so safe ,so rewarding, or so enjoyable, as it has been over the latter half of the last century, nor I believe will it ever be the same again. People now in their early years of retirement have enjoyed all the benefits of technology developed in a world war which they were too young to participate in, and the scientific achievements of a space race which they could only marvel at. With their formative years conditioned by austerity, they grew up to appreciate luxuries which are now regarded as necessities in the throw away society of today. There was an appreciation of what is right and what is wrong, a sense of justice for all, and punishment for the wrongdoer. There were recognised values and a comfortable pace to life governed by morals and the customs and culture of a country which had a confidence in the future and hope for future generations. Marriage and family life, the very cornerstones of our society, were still regarded as sacrosanct, and self respect, self control, fidelity, tolerance and politeness were still watchwords for a way of life which brought it's own reward. We have been able to buy our homes after a lifetime of hard work and dedication, and live comfortably on index linked pensions.
This was as it would always be. There would always be an England. Or so we thought.

Sadly enough it seems these attributes, and the Island heritage that sustained them, have long since been overtaken. A great many things have changed for the better but I wish I could be more optimistic about our future. Britain has horrendous problems now. The society that was has been transformed into the society it is. We need to ask ourselves whether we really are on the road to anarchy, and more importantly, if we are what, if anything, can we do about it. I believe the silent majority of our citizens are disgusted when criminal's rights are considered before those of the victims.. They are appalled at the breakdown of authority, shocked at the non existence of justice, and amazed at the farcical courts and judiciary which administer it. Without law and order we have nothing to aspire to. No wonder so many of us are moving abroad. World turmoil and the

unaccountable European Court of Human Rights has ensured that we are no longer in control of our own destiny, and with each year that passes we see more and more erosion of those things which have always been regarded as being British, and more importantly quintessentially English. The English dictionary defines the English as the natives or inhabitants of England, but sadly enough, in a roller coaster attempt to obliterate all things English, the last census form made no reference to the English race.
We are a rich country and we pride ourselves on living in a democratic society with the privilege of free speech. Like other rich countries, we should do everything possible to help the poorer nations of the world, but surely it is not racist to discuss how we might restrict illegal immigration. Surely it is not wrong to discuss measures which will not only secure our own future, and the status of those legal immigrants who have contributed so much to our society, but also those who may wish to legally enter and contribute even more to our society in the future. Surely the time has come to defend the borders of our small and densely populated island as we had no hesitation in doing in two world wars at a huge cost in British lives.

Why are we so ready to accept the immediate demands of equality campaigners, politically correct do-gooders, liberal radical reformers and the faceless politicians of a European Parliament, when they are not in our best interests. Why are such vital matters not open to general debate, and for that matter, why do we show such a degree of reluctance about anything English. In all matters relevant to British policies, the Scots now regard themselves as Scottish and the Welsh see themselves as Welsh. Both seem likely to remain so as we witness the gradual disintegration of the United Kingdom through the process of devolved government and regionalisation. At a time when other European Nations take action against anything which is not in their interests and many other countries in the world are seeking their own independence and a National sense of identity, we are slowly losing ours as we sleepwalk into oblivion. We are slowly losing the sense of who we really are. Other European countries are proud of their national heritage and resort to extreme measures to maintain their culture. Why don't we. Where has the National sentiment gone. I see few if any of those white flags with the red cross being flown on the day of our patron saint. Why is it not a National holiday. Why do we have to wait four years and the arrival of the world Cup to show any sign of national fervour and togetherness. Are we not proud of our land of hope and glory. Are we not proud to be English. The Empire may not have been perfect but many of the countries that were once a part of it are far from perfect now. It seems that England, Harry and St George are being further consigned to the history books with each year that passes and cool Britannia is slowly sinking beneath the very waves it once

ruled over.
Despite the wishes of the great majority of the people I believe the European Union's new constitution and with it the Euro, will eventually be thrust upon us anyway, and with it's introduction the last vestiges of our independency will be slowly but inevitably absorbed into a greater European Superstate. Sadly enough, in fifty years time, we may not be a Nation at all and, like the Polynesians of fifty years ago, our culture may well be a thing of the past.

How times have changed in the past fifty years. We have far more possessions now but many would claim that we also have a poorer quality of life. The blind may see and the lame may walk, but how ironic it is that whilst medical science has ensured that we live longer and technological progress has allowed us to work less hours, the over liberal and politically correct pendulum has swung too far for societies own good. Fed as we are on a daily diet of false promise, pornography and gratuitous violence, we now worship at the altar of materialism and instant gratification with little regard for the future. I worry for my children and their children growing up in a sick society where anything seems to be acceptable. Exposed as they are to constant images of virtual reality on television and lurid video games, their active formative minds must find it increasingly difficult to separate fact from fiction or right from wrong.
Our society is not only being changed, but it is being changed at an utterly bewildering rate. I am keenly aware that each older generation expresses concern as to what the world is coming to, and each succeeding generation believes theirs is an improvement on the last, but I do believe there has never been a time before when there has been more concern for the future. Before the second world war John F. Kennedy, the future president of the United States, wrote his book 'While England Slept', and the consequences of our slumber resulted in the greatest upheaval in our history. We are sleeping now and, oblivious to the enormous changes that are occurring in our society, I fear that unless we wake up soon, the consequences for our tiny Island will be even greater and we will see the end of all that is preserved of the past.

June never did throw down the gauntlet of domestic chores when I retired, neither did I take up the culinary challenge. I still do a bit of ironing from time to time though. Shirts are a problem, but there's something quite satisfying in getting a fine looking crease in crumpled trousers with the aid of a hot iron and a damp handkerchief. Must be my National service training. As a five year old senior citizen I sometimes find myself wondering how on earth I found the time to practice my profession before retirement. I still cannot find the time to do all the things I planned to do in my 'golden years'.

It's difficult to resist the temptation of cut price matinee seats at the local cinema complex of course, but when I'm not writing or struggling to master the intricacy of my computer, the multi purpose power drill and electric screwdriver are my new tools of trade now. I have a mammoth collection of plugs and screws but often lack the patience to find out how they all relate to one another. Since DIY and assembly of those irritating flat packs has never been one of my strong points I can never guarantee complete success, and since I often find myself doing more filling than drilling I must confess to wielding them more in hope than anticipation. Looking back I have always been more artistic than scientific, happier with a paint brush than a spanner. Must be the artist in me.
After wearing a more formal collar and tie during my working life I must confess that I find the current more demeaning dress code quite agreeable in retirement. Despite the odd protest from June there are few occasions to dress up for now. Like most men I've always been more inclined to dress down, but in deference to my more mature years I have recently drawn the line at the back to front baseball cap. Clothes may make the man impressive but there's few impressions left to make now.
My pressed suit and dinner jacket have long since been consigned to the back of my wardrobe in favour of more casual slacks and tee shirt. My shaving mirror will tell me what none of my friends will but, in keeping with my more secluded lifestyle, I shave less frequently now. In an effort to give myself a new image and look much younger I recently gave up shaving altogether, but the beard I grew was white and I looked much older.

Priorities have changed of course. No more thoughts of white water rafting in the Andes, trekking in the Himalayas or snowboarding in the Alps for me now. Any frivolous pretensions I may have had for such activities have long since evaporated. The insurance company would be appalled.
Once considered more mundane, some tasks completed in the past in a rare window of opportunity have assumed a whole new importance now. In the new order of things row, row, row, has been overtaken by mow, mow, mow. Maintenance work, gardening and cleaning have taken on a whole new meaning in the Summer months. They must be completed regularly and meticulously. Never before have the cut lines on the lawn looked so precise or the wheels on the car gleamed so brightly. In the grand scheme of things earlier serious discussion on cost control, liquidated damages and extensions of time, have now been replaced by small talk of fence posts, border plants and squeegee brushes.
Then of course there's the image thing. It's quite common in the elderly male I gather. In the best tradition of the search for a degree of lost youth, I continue to mix it with the best of them to prove to myself that I am still a

force to be reckoned with, and to convince others that the little grey cells and other bits and pieces are still in reasonable working order and I am still alive and kicking.

Life is a learning curve and a great teacher, but we often learn about it the hard way. Some learn slowly, but sadly enough, some don't learn about it at all. Only in later years did I begin to realise that change for it's own sake is not always for the better and necessity is not always the mother of invention, that small is beautiful and everything in life has a purpose. I have learned that if you have nothing to say you should say nothing, and if you have something to say you should say it. Experience teaches us what's worth doing is worth doing well and it is true that you cannot be all things to all men. In my more reflective moments I regret that I have not done many of the things I should have done and done many things I should not have done. I wish I had enjoyed the more pleasurable moments in life more, but strangely enough looking back, I recall their anticipation often proved to be better than their realisation. Conversely many matters of great concern at the time never materialised.
I have had a fair share of sea, sun and sangria, but I still have books to read and places to see. I have no wish to press the fast forward button. Having seen many of the lesser wonders of the world in my own country I sometimes wish that I had seen more of the greater wonders of the world in others. I reflect on the countries and the places I have visited and regret that I did not have the opportunity to visit more. The Taj Mahal at dawn, the Grand canyon at mid day, Ayers Rock in the evening and the Manhattan skyline at night. Perhaps I will one day.
At other times I recall the many people I have known from all walks of life, young and old alike. Characters who have influenced me in some way. I feel sure I have taken something that I have admired in them and inadvertently added it to my own personality over the years. I think we all do.

Seventy is perhaps a little too early to dwell too much on what I may have achieved in life and perhaps too late to start thinking of the after life - if there is one. My heart would like to think there is some form of spiritual or metaphysical being but on occasion my head thinks more rationally. Sadly enough with less than three per cent of the Church of England currently attending church, such irreverent thoughts would appear to be shared by the great majority of the population. In our so-called Christian country where is the Christian practice. Sunday service is associated more with the service at the local pub than the service at the local church. You don't need to go to church to prove you are a good Christian but it does help you to keep in touch with the ten commandments. If the nation still believes in a

supernatural power then it certainly does not wear it's religion on it's sleeve. I wonder sometimes if there is anyone out there. It's easy to philosophise. There are more conundrums in the vastness of the universe than our philosophy could ever dream of. Perhaps we are all Martians at heart anyway, but if there are any other little green men or extra terrestrials out there, why haven't they contacted us before now I wonder. Perhaps there is a cycle to humanity progressing to the point where it destroys itself and the life cycle starts again. There are many who would claim that the count down to Armageddon began way back in 1945 when the atomic bomb was dropped on Hiroshima, and it is only a matter of time before we blow ourselves up. It is impossible to prove such a conjecture, but given today's global arsenal of weapons of mass destruction it is easy to be pessimistic and postulate such a doomsday theory.
More pointedly, most of those that do attend church are in their retirement years and are probably more concerned about their health than the existence of aliens. In this respect I am no exception. Only after a life time of taking bodily and mental health for granted, and being fortunate enough to do so, have I come to truly appreciate just how remarkable a machine the human body is. Honed to perfection over millions of years it is truly an astonishing creation. I'm not a hypochondriac by nature, but any aches and pains now prompt an early reference to the household medical encyclopaedia to determine the cause, but I invariably become distracted by the symptoms of a whole host of other ailments and I forget what I was originally looking for. A little knowledge can be an unnerving thing.

I go back to the office occasionally to see old friends and colleagues and sometimes meet the young fresh faced new arrivals, their ambitions as yet undaunted by the pitfalls of the real world. When I do I suffer an initial tinge of regret at the thought of never being a part of the action again, but the feeling passes when I appreciate just how much I have forgotten about the stresses and strains of my former career, and just how much technology has moved on in Architecture in those five years since my retirement. Computer aided design, producing virtual reality drawings, has long since replaced the traditional drawing board, tee square and slide rule. In time honoured tradition they tell me how well I am looking, in much the same way as I have told other retired colleagues before me when I have noted how upright the stance, how alert and active, how firm the handshake and how clear the eye, and I hope they find the same in me.
At such times I think back to all the situations I had found myself in, some more serious or hazardous than others, and I tell them I put my survival down to my family genes, a happy marriage, attention to detail, and a rather large slice of luck. They enquire about my latest book, how I am enjoying

myself and we talk of plans for the future. I tell them it is always later than you think and I assure them that procrastination is the thief of time, that the past is history, the future uncertain and for those of any age only the present really matters.
Is this not true for all of us. In this uncertain world who knows what tomorrow might bring.

# 20. A GENERATION OF CHANGE - AND A BIT OF HISTORY

*I guess we could call ourselves survivors. Born before the second world war and the consequences of the baby boom which followed it, I and my generation have surely witnessed greater changes than have ever occurred in any previous lifetime. Changes and inventions that would have earlier been considered to be beyond belief are now a part of our everyday lives. Exiting as these changes and inventions may be I sometimes wonder whether they have totally improved our lot in life or added greatly to the sum of human happiness.*

*We have also witnessed changes that have brought a whole new meaning to the English language. The often baffling text messages we receive over our mobile phones are a measure of a whole new means of communication in our topsy turvy world and give a whole new meaning to the generation gap. As our use of the English language has changed then so to has the meaning of many words in an English dictionary which claims to be precise in every meaning of English words. Old words, new words, change of use words, it's all happened in the last century. Before our very eyes fiction has become fact and fact has become fiction in our new world of virtual reality. Whilst some words are hardly the Queen's English they have all been recognised as a part of the English language. Confused, then read on....*

❖

We were born before television, penicillin, radar, credit cards, polio shots, frozen food, Xerox, contact lenses, frisbees and the pill. Before radar, credit cards, split atoms, laser beams and ball point pens. Before panty hose, dishwashers, clothes dryers, electric blankets, air conditioners, drip dry clothes and flower power, before man walked on the moon and moonlighting was a job on the side.

We can recall when childhood, like the warm summer days, seemed to last forever. We played in the countryside in flower meadows, and fields of flora and fauna and long grass. We looked for bird's nests in overgrown hedgerows which teemed with insect life and, oblivious to the nettle stings on arms and legs, we chased a profusion of coloured butterflies. When you laid

back and closed your eyes it was possible to hear the hum of a multitude of invisible bumble bees. Sadly enough, it's all gone now, all sacrificed to fertilisers and high tech farming in the interests of cheap food.
We remember the steady drone of a monoplane high in a cloudless blue sky and skylarks singing on the wing on windy days, the rhythmic ticking of a clock in an otherwise silent room, the squelch underfoot of waterlogged grass, the discomfort of wet feet, the thrill of sliding on frozen lakes and the novelty of walking on ice covered mud. We recall the joy of an overnight snowfall and the satisfaction of making the first steps in it, the irritation of coming home after school on washdays to find clothes horses draped with steaming clothes, the reassurance in the warmth and glow of an open coal fire in the bedroom at times of illness, and cosy Saturday nights spent listening to the wireless swaddled in a dressing gown after a hot bath. We remember silent trolley buses and policemen on point duty, ploughs pulled by horses, belfast sinks, cold slabs and fly paper, fireguards and fenders, tablecloths and leaded lights and, typical of the older generation, we tend to confuse the songs of Karaoke with the actions of Karate.

The difference between the sexes had long been discovered by the time we arrived, and we did so before a sex change was possible. We came before cosmetic surgery was available to regain lost youth and viagra was obtainable to recover youthful pleasures. We were quite content to make do with what we had been equipped with when we arrived, and we were certainly the last generation to believe that only a husband and wife could adopt a child, or that a woman required a husband before she could have a baby.
We believed that a toy boy was an inactive doll to be played with by a child and not an active younger man to be played with by an older woman, far out was something seen at a distance and not something bizarre, and hands on was the opposite of hands off. Time sharing meant togetherness and not part ownership of a property, big girls blouse referred to an outsize ladies garment, a chip meant a small piece of wood, hardware meant metal tools, and software was a word yet to appear in an English dictionary.
My generation did the right thing. They deemed it correct to get married first and live together afterwards. Those that didn't lived in sin and not cohabitation. Closets were for clothes and not for something to come out of. Bunnies were small pet rabbits and not girls dressed as rabbits, Designer Jeans were scheming women named Jean, and a flasher was someone who operated a signalling lamp rather than a man showing his credentials.

Fast food for my generation was what you ate during lent, and made in Japan meant a cheap imitation, Pizza House, McDonalds, Kentucky Fried

Chicken, and the instant coffee sold in them, were unheard of. The veggieburger had yet to arrive as a variant of the hamburger, a joint was something to eat at Sunday lunchtime and not a cannabis cigarette to smoke at any time, and a chip was a thin strip of fried potato enjoyed with fish and not a part of an electrical circuit.
We lived at a time when a mouse was a long tailed rodent which caused women of all ages to jump on to tables and chairs in a frenzy and not a controller device attached to a computer, when heavy metal was a high density chemical element and not a high density rock music, when a flat top was an aircraft carrier and not a head with the hair cut short on the top, and a time before decimal currency, when a small piece of green paper was a pound note - small change by today's decimal standards. We came before house husbands, gay rights, computer dating, dual careers and computer marriages. Before day care centres, group therapy and nursing homes, FM Radio, tape decks, electric typewriters, word processors, artificial hearts and yogurt, and before guys wore earrings and gals wore trousers.

We were around when Woolworths was referred to as the threepenny and sixpenny store and for that amount you could buy fish and chips at your local chippy, a couple of bottles of Pepsi at the corner shop, and enough stamps for three letters at a village post office. We have witnessed the demise of branded goods that are no longer manufactured. Brands that were once household names. Radiant and Omo washing powders, Five Boys chocolate, Sharp's toffees, Jubbly ice cream and Fry's Tiffin Bars, Horniman's and Tower tea, Sifta salt and Flag sauce, VP ruby wine, Passing Cloud Cigarettes, Astral soap and Hepworth's made to measure men's suits. All now long gone the way our culture is rapidly going.
We remember crisp packets and the excitement of discovering the small twist of blue paper containing the salt inside, fireplaces and fireguards, coal scuttles and coalmen, door to door brush salesmen and outside school toilets, which froze up in winter and smelled in the Summer. We can recall a time when cigarette smoking was fashionable and grass was something to be mowed, coke was a cold drink, pot was something to cook food in, Aids were regarded as helpers and rock music was a lullaby. We can remember when an iron curtain was a protective metal grille and not a guarded border between two countries, and more onerously when a shooting gallery was something to be found at a fairground and not on National Health Service premises where drug addicts can freely inject themselves with free heroin. We remember when it was fashionable to give gifts of slippers and ties or cardigans and gloves at Christmas, when the recipients would declare that they were just what they wanted.

It is difficult to pick out the most memorable events or the most notable achievements that have occurred in my lifetime, and almost impossible to chose the most distinguished and glamorous celebrities of my generation. A few however do spring readily to mind.
If organ transplants were a huge advance in the medical world, then the jumbo jet was largely responsible for shrinking it. If space satellites transformed communication, then computers were around to exploit it. If situation comedy with the likes of Only Fools and Horses and Fawlty Towers has done a lot to lighten our lives, then The Today Programme has done even more to enlighten our minds. If the automatic washing machine has reduced domestic chores, then central heating has provided domestic comfort. The likes of Winston Churchill was around to guide us through times of adversity, Morecambe and Wise to make us laugh, Frank Sinatra to keep us entertained, the 1966 World cup to make the boys happy, and waterproof mascara to keep the girls beautiful.

Some innovations and advances in science, medicine and technology, have been more notable than others, some were taken for granted in the name of scientific progress, but each decade brought it's own achievement to transform the way we lived.
The optimistic fabulous Fifties brushed away the cobwebs of the post war years of austerity and gave women an air of respectability when they drank 'Babycham' in a public bar. There was still respect for authority and Britain was still great. Our spirits soared to the pomp and ceremony of the Coronation, and the achievement of Hillary and Tensing when they conquered Everest. We saw the first commercial flight of a jet aircraft called the Comet, the first animal to enter space named Laika, and the introduction of the Morris Mini which was even smaller than the Morris Minor. For the first time in our history we watched history being made on our television set. We changed channels with a remote control, but when we started to eat our labour saving dinners in front of it, the days when the entire family sat down together for a home made meal were already numbered.
Things went with a swing in the liberating swinging sixties. The decade began with the introduction of the electron microscope, and ended with Neil Armstrong taking his one small step for man on the moon with the world watching in awe as satellite television relayed the live pictures. In a ten year cycle of social change when we were told not to drink and drive and that paper pants would be the conventional unmentionables of the future, we saw the introduction of the home kidney dialysis machine and the life saving implanted pacemaker, and witnessed the introduction of the life impeding pill.
The seventies were memorable for the introduction of watches with LCD

displays, pocket calculators which didn't fit in the pocket, cars with air bags you never hoped to see, and bar code readers you couldn't understand. The decade also gave us the prawn cocktail as an aperitif and Blue Nun wine to wash it down. The birth of the home computer, gave rise to a whole new dictionary of jargon which baffled all but the computer boffin, whilst the more controversial conception by IVF did much the same for those who wished for offspring.

Came the Eighties, came the baked potato. DNA fingerprinting was as helpful in combating crime rates as prozac was to those suffering depression, and video keyhole surgery an unbelievable innovation for those with more life threatening disorders. In a decade of ostentation and power the internet, the lap top computer and dot com reigned supreme.

Alcops became the fashionable drink of the nineties which was all about style, sex and sleaze, spurred on by satellite, cable, digital television and internet browsing, in a world of instant communication and instant gratification. We marvelled at the cloning of dolly the sheep but recoiled when it raised the spectre of carbon copy humans made to order. In the interests of space exploration the first section of the International space station was launched shortly after Buzz Lightyear made his appearance. In the interests of healthy eating we had our first taste of Frankenstein food in the form of genetically modified tomatoes, and in the interests of those throughout the world without electricity we came up with the clockwork radio.

Sadly it was also the decade which saw the tragic death of Princess Diana in a horrendous car crash in Paris, and many less than palatable allegations against the Royal Household. The questionable manipulations and dubious protocol of the palace may have brought her despair in life, but it seems that she done more to damage their reputation in death. The more Republican minded in the country must be gloating. On a lighter note, in confirmation of her popularity, and the fact that the younger generation seem to recall historic events seen on television more readily than those they read in history books, it is a date many of them regard as the most significant of the last century.

There we have it. So much for the lifetime of my generation. A lifetime of change. Some for the good, some for the not so good. Our lives have become more pressurised and frustrated now we struggle to keep up with the state of the art technology. Faced with an embarrassment of choice we feel obliged to live in the fast lane without knowing when to apply the brakes. We may be more permissive but I doubt that we are more civilised. In material terms, life in our society is far easier now than it was fifty years ago, but many of our problems are a result of our materialistic society. So much expected, so much anticipated and so much taken for granted in a world now regrettably rich in moralists but poor on morality.

I'm sure I and my generation have lived in the best of times. Had I known fifty years ago just how good the next fifty years would be, I'm sure I would have looked forward to them more. But what of the next fifty. Assuming a six mile wide rogue asteroid doesn't strike our planet and do for us what one did for the dinosaurs sixty five million years ago, or some misguided terrorist organisation, dismissive of our western way of life, fails to develop a suitcase sized nuclear weapon, or we haven't poisoned ourselves by eating genetically modified food, what sort of future might they hold. What sort of liberty and what sort of attributes will prevail in our intended multi cultural society if we don't all drown as a result of global warming or we are all not wiped out by a global epidemic I wonder. Hopefully a future not too dehumanised and devoid of humanity after attempting to clone the best of ourselves through genetic manipulation, but one in which we can truthfully say things are getting better.

Though I won't be around to witness it, perhaps mankind will finally realize it's potential for good rather than it's inclination toward evil. After all as we would all like to believe, the day dreams of yesterday often become the hopes of today and the reality of tomorrow. But don't count on it. All men are created equal, but some will always believe that they have been created more equal than others......